Hand In Hand

An Autobiographical Novel

Hand In Hand

An Autobiographical Novel

››››‹‹‹‹

Written by Rashel Veprinski
Translated by Ellen Cassedy and Anita Norich

Hand in Hand: An Autobiographical Novel
By Rashel Veprinski
Translated by Ellen Cassedy and Anita Norich

White Goat Press, the Yiddish Book Center's imprint
Yiddish Book Center
Amherst, MA 01002
whitegoatpress.org

Printed in the United States of America at The Studley Press, Dalton, MA
10 9 8 7 6 5 4 3 2 1

Paperback ISBN 979-8-9909980-9-4
Ebook ISBN 979-8-9987798-0-0

Library of Congress Control Number: 2025937369

Book design by Michael Grinley
Cover design by Kandy Littrell
Cover photograph: Jeannine McChesney/RooM via Getty Images

This book was made possible with generous support from the children of Rabbi Emanuel S. Goldsmith in memory of their father and teacher, editor of Yiddish Literature in America 1870-2000.

Translators' Introduction

Hand in Hand is an intimate portrait of a passionate romance that takes place in New York at the beginning of the 20th century. The novel's two central characters are based on the author, Rashel Veprinski, and her partner of more than thirty years, Mani Leyb, a lyric poet who was a leader of their Yiddish literary circle, known as *Di Yunge* [the youth]. The title (*Dos kreytsn fun di hent* in Yiddish) comes from a poem by Mani Leyb, which appears in a letter to Veprinski along with several other letters in the novel.

First published in Yiddish in 1971, *Hand in Hand* takes place in 1918, beginning with the first encounter between Miriam (Veprinski) and Nyezhiner (Mani Leyb, "the man from Nyezhin," today Nizhyn, a city in Ukraine). Although the novel keeps its focus on the inner lives of the couple and the doings of their circle, the city comes alive in all its "rhythmic thrum." Miriam's multigenerational immigrant family comes into view. We see the constant struggle against poverty and illness, the challenges of immigration and assimilation, the pressures on women during a time of changing mores, the erotic pleasure the couple experiences. There are vivid portraits of gatherings in cafés and apartments. A summer in the lush Catskill Mountains north of New York provides welcome relief from the heat and pressures of the city, even as the couple's struggles continue.

Miriam has always "longed for something . . . that had yet to be revealed, a secret something that was waiting for her. She wanted to be free to discover that secret." Like the poetic movement of which Mani Leyb and Veprinski were a part, Nyezhiner offers Miriam a window into the beauty that can be found in even the grittiest surroundings. "The world is a lovely place," he promises, and the pair seeks that beauty together.

Arising in the first decade of the twentieth century when New York Yiddish culture was flourishing, *Di Yunge* sought to distinguish themselves from earlier poets, especially the so-called sweatshop poets whom the poet Zishe Landau, one of *Di Yunge*, dismissed as "the rhyme department of the Jewish labor movement." As Reuben Iceland, another member of *Di Yunge*, wrote: "We proclaimed the freedom of poetry and its right to an independent life. We maintained that poetry should not exist by reason of whatever ideas it has, because it lives for its own sake . . . We threw out social themes . . . We avoided national motifs . . . We realized that to properly express intimate, lyrical feelings, we must . . . search within ourselves . . ."* Like the characters in this novel, the members of *Di Yunge* were quarrelsome and competitive but also deeply engaged with one another. They were working-class intellectuals and aesthetes who toiled for long hours in factories, restaurants, and stores; supported their families; dealt with serious illnesses; gathered for long bouts of conversation; pursued love affairs; broke up and reunited; and spent many hours reading their works to one another. They published a succession of little magazines, most of which lasted for only a few issues.

The author describes the book as "an autobiographical novel." It is unquestionably a roman à clef (literally a "novel with a key" in

---

*Iceland, Reuven, *From Our Springtime: Literary Memoirs and Portraits of Yiddish New York*, translated by Gerald Marcus (Syracuse: Syracuse University Press, 2013), pp. 6–8. (Originally published as *Fun un[d]zer friling* [New York: Inzl, 1954]).

which known historical figures are presented). It is tempting to try to figure out which character in the novel is based on which real personality. In some cases it is clear who is who. The "blond poet" with whom Nyezhiner is often at odds is Moyshe Leyb Halpern. "Yankev Shor" is the poet Reuben Iceland. "Ada," Shor's lover, is Rosa Lebensboym (aka Anna Margolin). In many cases, however, the author seems to have mixed and matched attributes of real people in creating the novel's panoply of colorful characters.

Although the novel was published in Yiddish more than fifty years after the events it describes, it reads as if it were written as the events unfolded. Everything about it is precise and sharp, its language spare and natural. Sometimes scathing, sometimes gently humorous, Veprinski reveals her characters' doubts, insecurities, and passion for Yiddish literature and for one another.

››››‹‹‹‹

« CHAPTER 1 »

THEY WALKED toward the Williamsburg Bridge, Miriam by his side. Even with her hat on, she barely reached his shoulder, yet they walked at a steady pace, matching their steps. Nyezhiner raised his hand in the air.

"How can it be?" he asked. They'd lived near each other for two years in Williamsburg yet never met. "It's unbelievable!"

Miriam looked up at him. Softly, warmly, his gray eyes met hers. Their walking together, with him holding her arm, was unexpected but somehow not surprising. It was as if their walking arm in arm on this lovely evening had been determined long ago.

They joined the crowd on Clinton Street. Tall tenements rose up on both sides, blocking the sky. The street was full of horse-drawn carts and manure. A car honked and children made a racket. It was still light out, but the gas lamps had been turned on, and the bright shop windows displayed lingerie, corsets, stylish hats, wedding clothes to buy or rent.

On the stoops sat women in wigs and kerchiefs who looked as if they were just off the boat. They gazed at everything as if in a dream.

Miriam made her way through the crowd with small dainty steps. Her clothes and her bearing made her look as if she'd come from uptown to see the slums.

Nyezhiner bent down to her, his face aglow. “How do you like all this, our Jewish tumult, eh?” he asked. “Isn’t it amazing that children manage to grow up here? And with color in their cheeks, too! Miraculous!”

“Miraculous?” said Miriam, smiling. “Then I must be a miracle too. I grew up near here, on Avenue B.”

“Really?”

“Right off the ship,” she said. “My mother was a widow, and I was the youngest of four. I walked on this street all the time and looked in the shop windows with envy.”

“Really? On Avenue B!”

“Yes, the same Avenue B you celebrate in your poems.”

“Well . . . in one of my very early works.”

Miriam looked at him curiously. Something in his tone seemed apologetic, as if he’d long since outgrown that early poem, but she wasn’t sure. She’d always liked the poem, knew it practically by heart. She knew all his shorter poems by heart, having read them in newspapers and journals. And, indeed, that was how Ada had introduced the two of them earlier that evening.

“Meet one of your readers: Miriam Eidelberg. She knows all your poems by heart!” And Ada’s small blue eyes had twinkled with laughter, her bosom swelling with pride. It was she who brought Miriam all the newspapers and journals that published *Di Yunge*, the young Yiddish poets. Ada was the leading lady of Yiddish literature.

Miriam had felt embarrassed, like a child whose clever words were repeated to strangers.

Nyezhiner had looked at her. “I’ll bet you write poems, too.” When Miriam laughed, he added, “Such a pretty laugh.”

Since then he hadn’t left her side. Now he was walking her home, and Ada, who had brought her to the poetry reading a few hours earlier, had blown her a kiss and stayed on East Broadway to go to a café with Nyezhiner’s colleague Yankev Shor.

They came to the bridge, whose white stone steps beckoned them up to the promenade. Underneath, a tangle of streetcars ran back and forth to Brooklyn.

"Come. Let's walk across. It's not far. You must have done it often if you live in Williamsburg."

"But never the whole way," Miriam confessed with a guilty smile. "On a nice day, I often walk partway across with my daughter. She likes to look at the water, the barges, the ships."

"You have a child!" Nyezhiner tried to read her expression by the light of the street lamp. Her face seemed childishly young, the skin smooth, with little written upon it. He wanted to draw a finger over that smoothness, to touch the lashes that hid her dark eyes.

"Come," he said, taking the lead. "I'll show you New York at night, when it's all lit up."

He took her arm and they went up the stone steps, even though it was time for her to hurry home and tell Dinaleh her bedtime story. The child was waiting.

It was Miriam's first time up on the bridge in the evening. No one was about. A cool breeze wafted over her face, and a musty dampness emanated from the river as it flowed between stone embankments. A barge crept along, slow as a turtle. In the distance, the Brooklyn Bridge hung like a spider web. The windows of the skyscrapers glittered with a cold, flickering light.

They stood without speaking. Then Nyezhiner pointed at the city. "Well, what do you say? Do you like it?"

Miriam didn't know what to say. Whenever she'd viewed this scene through the streetcar windows, the flickering lights had struck her as cold and unwelcoming.

"It's beautiful," she said, "but a bit eerie, don't you think?"

Nyezhiner agreed. It occurred to him that maybe this was precisely why he came here so often: just to feel, again and again, the uncanny hugeness of the city, its enormous strangeness.

He took her arm again and they walked on in silence. How

odd, Miriam thought, that this person she'd just met, with whom she'd spoken for the very first time today, should seem both familiar and unfamiliar, like a long-lost relative.

Nyezhiner stopped to light a cigarette and leaned on the railing. "Are you tired?" he asked. He gestured at a bench. "Shall we sit?"

"No, thank you." She was not at all tired and didn't want to sit down. But her high-heeled shoes were hurting her. She'd worn them because she hadn't expected to be walking. She leaned on the railing beside him, standing first on one foot and then on the other, rotating her slender ankles like a ballet student practicing her moves.

Nyezhiner had noticed her lemon-yellow shoes, how they laced up, how they creased softly at the ankles. He liked looking at a well-made shoe on a pretty foot and paid particular attention to the quality of the stitching.

"You're wearing deerskin shoes," he said, "and you wear them well!"

Miriam giggled. A memory flashed into her mind. When she was fifteen, a boy had complimented her shoes. But "deerskin"! Only a poet would use such a word.

She took his arm. "Let's go," she said. "My heels aren't hurting anymore, and I should have been home long ago. My daughter is waiting for her bedtime story."

Nyezhiner walked quietly at her side, shortening his steps to match hers. Her bright yellow shoes flashed beside his dark ones as if whispering a secret.

"You look like a child," he said, breaking the silence, "but you already have a child. How did you manage that?"

"How did I manage it?" Miriam said. "What do you mean? Any woman can have a child at seventeen or eighteen or even earlier. But I'm not sure it's a good thing. Should a child have a mother who never had a girlhood? A mother who wishes she were still a girl herself?"

She stopped, afraid she'd said too much. She rarely spoke about herself, even with people she knew well. And here she was confiding in a virtual stranger, walking with him arm in arm across the bridge as if they were parading across a red carpet while her child waited for her at home.

Nyezhiner felt her hidden sadness. He'd known at first sight that she wasn't happy; he could always sense such things. He was drawn to unhappy women. In Miriam, though, he saw not so much an unhappy woman as a young girl whose restlessness had no name, her longing no object; and there arose in him a kind of elegiac song, an echo that sang to him of something he had missed out on and would never have. At thirty-three, he already felt well into his autumn years. His youth was over and done with, lost and gone away . . . A line of a poem passed through his mind like a ray of light and disappeared. He shivered and took Miriam's hand in both of his, once more looking at her face in the moonlight.

"My God! You're just a child yourself," he said, "yet you're already burdened with motherhood."

Miriam pulled her hand away. He had touched on something that bothered her deeply. She would gladly sacrifice herself for Dinaleh. She was devoted to her child. Yet she had decided not to have any more children even though David wanted them. She wanted to study, to travel, to write, to learn all about the world. Would she want all this even if she were married to someone other than David? She didn't know.

She turned toward Nyezhiner. "You were very young when you became a father, too," she said. "Ada told me, and I can see from your poems that the responsibilities of fatherhood weigh on you. What is it like to have to support five children and then . . ."

Miriam was surprised by her own audacity. How many times had she asked him these questions in her mind, even before meeting him? Now the questions came tumbling out, and she wanted to ask more: Why had he fallen out of love so quickly with the other woman, the one for whom he'd left his wife and children? But of course she wouldn't ask him, no matter how badly she wanted to know. How strange that his personal life mattered so much to her. As soon as Ada had told her that her favorite poet, whom she'd never even met, had left his wife and children for another woman, she'd found herself feeling personally involved, even jealous. She still didn't understand why.

Nyezhiner looked at her, taken aback, then offered a small smile. After all, he reflected, he had struck an intimate tone with her, so he shouldn't be surprised by her questions.

"I won't go into all that now," he said quietly. "Maybe another time. You seem to know a lot more about my personal life than I imagined."

"Oh, I know very little. Only what I hear from Ada. And a word here and there from people who are curious about the lives of poets and artists."

Nyezhiner smiled bitterly. "Artists! Poets!" he scoffed. He laughed out loud. "The truth is, I'm an ordinary worker. I sit at a machine sewing uppers for women's shoes—fine shoes like yours. You see that stitch there? I'm a master of that seam, a true professional, probably the best in the business. But poems? Someone like me, someone with my talent, should stop fooling around with shoes and devote himself full time to writing. I mean it! Some of my friends don't work. They go hungry, but at least they aren't tied to a machine. I envy them, but I can't do that. I have five children, so I have to keep sewing shoes. It's the one thing I can do for them. Do you see? I'm responsible for them."

Miriam hung her head. Of course she understood there was no letting go of the responsibility for one's children. Ever. Suddenly she felt sorry—sorry for him and sorry for herself. In the lamplight he looked as tired as her brother Moyshe when he came home from the shop. In fact, she could see a resemblance between the two of them—both tall, both handsome.

On they walked, without talking, as if all that mattered was to keep walking. Miriam forgot herself, forgot that her shoes hurt.

She walked as if she had already outwalked all her troubles and now could walk all night. Suddenly she could hear the squealing of the streetcars in the plaza on the Brooklyn side of the bridge, and her eyes were dazzled by the oncoming headlights and the streaming light of restaurants, cafeterias, stores, all ablaze with signs.

"That was quick!" Miriam exclaimed. "I thought the bridge was much longer."

They made their way through the traffic and turned onto a quiet side street by the river.

"So this is where you live?" he asked.

"About five blocks away."

"In one of the new buildings?"

"Yes, it's two years old. We were among the first to move in."

"Two years ago," said Nyezhiner, "I was working here by the bridge. There used to be a lot of shoe factories here. Now they've moved deeper into Brooklyn, and these modern apartment buildings have taken their place. I used to hang around here for hours with my friends when there was no work. Brooklyn is horribly gray and monotonous, the streets endless, but we barely noticed. We walked around talking about poetry and yearning for the cities we came from, the familiar landscapes back home."

"There are beautiful cities here, too," Miriam said, coming to the defense of America and Brooklyn, "and beautiful streets. Ada lives not far from here in a wonderful old mansion that's been made into apartments. Her street is so wide, so beautiful."

"Yes, I know there are still some old streets full of beautiful old houses, but most of Brooklyn is just old, not beautiful."

"What about you?" Miriam asked. "Where in Brooklyn do you live?"

"You'll be disappointed to hear I live in the poor section, in a little furnished room. I don't even have a desk."

"Really? I have a desk I hardly ever use. You can have it."

"That's very kind," he said with a smile, "but my room isn't big enough. Not to mention that I've never actually used a desk. I used to love writing at the kitchen table, especially late at night, when everyone was asleep and the coals in the stove were still smoldering . . ."

Miriam imagined that kitchen, that table, when his wife and children were asleep. Lines from his poems came to mind, and now she understood them better. Sad, sad lines . . . and yet, could it be that now he was longing for those late hours at the kitchen table, warming himself with poems while his loved ones slept nearby? She wanted to ask: If he was lonely and the other woman who'd been the cause of it all was no longer with him, why didn't he go back to his family? But she wouldn't ask; it was none of her business.

Nyezhiner took her hands and bent to kiss them. "You're a good person, Miriam, I can tell. We've just met, but we've known each other for years. Am I right?"

Miriam didn't answer, but she agreed with him. He was right. They had known each other for years. His every gesture felt oddly familiar, like a scribbled line she knew she'd read before, without remembering where or when.

They arrived at a tidy brick building. "Here we are," said Miriam.

Nyezhiner noted the house number: 777.

"Will you come in? You're very welcome. David must be home from the pharmacy by now." She didn't say "my husband," but he understood. "You can meet my mother too. She's here tonight. You'll like her: all she ever reads is prayer books—never a single line of poetry."

"I like her already."

"So come up, won't you?"

"Another time, with pleasure."

"Next Friday? David is home early on Fridays."

"All right then, I'll be glad to."

"A special guest for Shabbos!" And Miriam quickly said goodbye and disappeared inside.

Nyezhiner remained standing in front of the building. He looked again at the address: 777. He didn't need to write it down. He would remember.

But maybe it would be better not to come next Friday, better not to see her again. He had a feeling that getting together would do her no favors. He had never made a woman happy. At that moment he felt a pang of pity for himself, for her, and for David, whom he didn't even know.

« CHAPTER 2 »

OUTSIDE A sparkling snow had begun to fall. The wind drove the flakes up into the air. Through the narrow window of the pharmacy, David could see them swirling. Amid his tins and bottles he mixed his powders, and his thoughts swirled like the snow.

Could he blame Miriam for spending so much time with Nyezhiner? No. Even he enjoyed himself whenever Nyezhiner came for supper. The man had a marvelous ability to draw even the most silent person into conversation. Evenings with Nyezhiner passed quickly, and afterward he always felt uplifted, more important in his own eyes. Truly, he had never met such an interesting and attractive person as this Nyezhiner. So why blame Miriam? Of course she felt honored when Nyezhiner came to visit. Besides, the man had no home. Miriam had even offered him her desk as a place to work.

David knew that while he was at the pharmacy, busy with his powders and prescriptions, Nyezhiner was visiting Miriam. She told him so herself: "Nyezhiner was here. He wrote something at the desk and read it to me."

And why not? Miriam was a good listener, and she read a lot. He couldn't remember when he himself had last picked up a book. Here in America, it fell to men to make a living. Women, especially those of the middle class, had a lot of free time. It was no accident that America had so many female writers. Miriam was drawn to writing too. He knew she had notebooks filled with her writing in her desk drawer. She'd never read any of it to him. She was highly secretive about her writing. But perhaps she read her writings to Nyezhiner. David felt the blood pounding in his temples at the thought. How could he compare himself to Nyezhiner?

One evening, when Nyezhiner and others were visiting, Miriam sang one of his songs. All the guests sang along. The melody and the words were simple and flowing. Afterward Nyezhiner smiled and said it was a weak poem. Everyone stared at him, surprised, and he launched into a talk about poetry that David didn't really understand. He wasn't sure Miriam understood it all either, even though she was always running to the library and coming home with armloads of poetry books, American and foreign. Lately she seemed livelier, happier. Before, she often seemed distracted, subdued, indifferent to her surroundings. He ought to be pleased that she had become so much more animated. But instead he felt very upset.

It wasn't the first time that thinking about Miriam had made him anxious. He remembered when his student friend Avrom used to come around in the evening. Avrom loved visiting. He was new to America but felt quickly at home. His older brother, a tailor, was paying for him to study. In the evenings when David came home from the pharmacy where he was then employed, he would often find Avrom already there; Miriam had invited him to stay for supper. Sometimes Avrom would take Miriam to the theater and David would stay home with their child. Or Miriam, who was then nineteen years old, would ask Avrom to take her ice skating in Central Park. They were living in Harlem then, and many of the young Jews spent their evenings at the rink. Miriam would come home with her face aglow, eyes shining. That's when he grew uneasy and felt as foolish as he did now. Back then he'd been angry with Miriam. If she wanted to get rid of him, why turn to Avrom?

How was Avrom any better than he was? True, Avrom had a certain cosmopolitan air that David lacked, but he was an impractical young man who hadn't yet found his way in life. Soon Avrom moved away to study in another city, and that's how things ended between them.

Now it was another story. He couldn't compare himself to Nyezhiner. He was in awe of the man, of his enormous talent and charm. He remembered Nyezhiner's first visit. Not every poet David met at literary soirees looked so dignified and handsome. He remembered thinking that evening that if Miriam decided to trade him in for this man, it wouldn't even bother him so much. But now that it seemed such a thing might actually happen, it did bother him, very much—much more than before, with Avrom. Back then he hadn't felt as distant from Miriam as he did now. He knew she and their child were at home, just a few blocks from the drugstore, yet she seemed miles away from where he stood with his bottles and pills and thoughts. Nyezhiner might be in their home even now. What if he were to come home and find them together? What then? The idea brought a sudden heat to his face, and he broke out in a sweat. Maybe he had a fever? There was a virus going around. He couldn't keep his mind on the prescriptions. Dinaleh had a cold, and Miriam had planned to keep her home from school. He really should go home and see how the child was doing. He'd bring some aspirin. Miriam would be surprised—he never came home so early. But he had a headache. Why was he having all these wild thoughts?

Suddenly his coat was on, a packet of aspirin in his pocket. He left the store, then tried the door. Yes, locked. But the notice saying he'd be back in ten minutes was still in his hand. He went back in and posted it in the window. It looked like a face gazing out at the street.

The snow had stopped, but the wind was still blowing the flakes into feathery drifts. The ground was white, the sky dark.

David walked with boyish pleasure. It felt good to trudge

through the drifts, breathing the fresh air. He whistled a bit as he walked. Sometimes whole days and even weeks went by when he didn't really know what the outdoors looked like. He just stood behind the counter thinking his crazy thoughts. Now, walking through the pristine snow, he felt embarrassed by his impure thoughts about Miriam.

How good to make his way through the crisp snow as the evening shadows crept up the walls. The air grew warmer, the sky darker. Maybe it would rain and the snow would be washed away. Too bad. He remembered the old country where the snow would stay on the ground until Passover, when the river thawed and the spring rains came.

David realized he had passed his house. As he retraced his steps, his pleasant mood disappeared. Somehow, going past his home and having to turn around seemed connected to Miriam's estrangement from him.

He opened the door to the building and climbed the stairs. The lights had not yet been turned on. The hallway was pitch black. He saw a shadow coming toward him. As they passed on the steps, they recognized each other. They stopped in their tracks, as wordless as if someone had grabbed them by the throat.

Nyezhiner wanted to turn back around and go to David, but his feet were leaden. How long did they stand there? A minute? An eternity? Finally David went up the steps to his apartment and opened the door.

It was dark in the apartment. David felt for the switch in the foyer and turned on the light. He went into the living room and saw Miriam sitting on the blue sofa, her face in her hands, her braids hanging down. On the coffee table stood a half-finished glass of tea. A cigarette was burning in the ashtray.

Miriam looked up and stared at him as if she were dreaming, not really seeing him. To her he looked enormous, his mouth twisted and bitter. He came closer, very close, then raised his hand and gave her face a hard slap. He turned away abruptly and went to the door. Miriam heard his heavy footsteps, the dreadful slamming of the door that rattled the dishes in the kitchen. She felt as if she were falling from a great height and would smash to pieces.

Dinaleh had awakened and now stood at the door of her room looking wide-eyed at her mother, at the tears rolling down her face. She didn't come closer. A dark, unfamiliar feeling held her back. She had never seen tears on her mother's face. How strange she looked!

Miriam wiped her tears. She realized the inevitable had happened. She was now alone with Dinaleh. She got up from the sofa.

"Come, Dinaleh, you had a long nap. It's time for supper. Ooh, my head hurts."

She went to Dinaleh, put her lips to her daughter's brow, felt how cool it was, and kissed her. Dinaleh seemed relieved and snuggled into her mother's arms.

Later, Dinaleh sat down at the piano. Every night after dinner she had to practice the pieces her teacher had assigned, but tonight she was actually eager to play. The ivory keys drew her little fingers like a magnet. The unusual stillness in the apartment seemed to make the notes ring clearer. She knew she was playing well. She turned to look for her mother's approving expression but instead noticed her anxious smile and the tears in her eyes. She took a long look at her mother and felt she was understanding something—but she didn't know what.

That evening Miriam put Dinaleh to bed later than usual because of her long nap. She started to tell her a story as she always did, but the words came out in a jumble. Lost in thought, she stopped in the middle of the story. Dinaleh whispered a bit to herself and fell asleep.

It grew even quieter in the apartment. From the direction of the East River, shrouded in fog, a siren wailed. Miriam lay down on the sofa still in her clothes. The hours dragged on as she waited for David to come back. She listened carefully and thought she heard his firm steps. What would he do when he returned? Kill her? No, she told herself, not that. He might not be in his right mind, but he wouldn't be able to make his hands do such a thing. More likely he would fall at her feet and weep and beg her to forgive him. She would need to tell him only that whatever he'd imagined between her and Nyezhiner had not actually happened. He would believe her. It was, after all, the truth. David must have met Nyezhiner on the staircase. Then he'd found her sitting in the dark. So . . . what else could he have thought?

The slap? She would not have believed David capable of it. But surely he would return looking miserable, crying and begging her to deny what he suspected. All she needed to tell him was that unexpectedly, in the middle of the snowstorm, Nyezhiner had knocked on the door. She'd opened it, surprised to see him in such weather. He'd apologized, explained that he'd gone to the shop but there was no work, her house was nearby, he didn't know what to do, was he disturbing her? No, no, she'd said, come in. She'd been doing housework and wanted to pin up her braids, but he told her to leave them down, they looked good on her. His compliment pleased her, and she left her braids down. She gave him tea, as usual. He took only a sip, warmed his hands on the hot glass, and began telling her about his short-lived but passionate affair with the woman for whom he'd left his wife and children. When it grew dark, he got up and left.

So simple. David would believe her. He would want to believe her. But in some deep place in himself he would know that what she was telling him was not so simple and not the whole truth, and he would no longer trust her as he had before. And, in truth, she wasn't planning to tell him everything. She would not actually tell him how glad she was when Nyezhiner found her with her braids down and saw her beautiful long hair. She would not tell him that she dreamed about Nyezhiner the night before. In the dream, they were very close, and he kissed her as no man had ever kissed her before.

She would not tell him that as the room grew dark they sat

quietly on the sofa, forgetting to turn on the light. Then he felt for her hand, kissed her palm, and didn't let go. There they sat in the dwindling light, forgetting about the time, until Dinaleh cried out in her sleep and awakened them both from their reverie. She went to Dinaleh, and when she came back he had his coat on. He said a quick good-bye and left the apartment. In his quick, light steps, she recognized that he was suddenly afraid David might arrive. He walked as softly and stealthily as a thief. She felt herself turning against him. How many secret affairs had he had? Just as she found herself beginning to dislike him, she disliked herself for being implicated in his thieving ways. Why had he told her about his love affair with that woman, whom he'd described as a kind of nymphomaniac? Was he trying to arouse her? To make her jealous? And had he? Maybe. She would certainly never see him again. He had disturbed her very soul. He was much older and had already loved several women and taken what he could from those loves: romance and whatever else he was looking for. On top of which, the fact that he had a wife and children, even though he didn't live with them, repelled her. She'd had no intention of making him her lover when she invited him in. It was simply an honor to be friends with a great poet whose poems she knew by heart. But now things had changed. He had awakened her erotic desires, and she was jealous of his former loves and even of his wife, whom he did not love but with whom he had five children.

No, she wouldn't tell David any of that. But she knew one thing. She and David had to separate. Their life together hadn't been good before and it certainly wouldn't be now. She would never forgive him for slapping her, and he would always suspect her of deceiving him. And she might do just that in time—learn to cheat on him. Not that she wanted to learn. Even though she couldn't bear it when David approached her in bed. That kind of life was no good for either of them. And they were both so young. Each of them had to build a new life, a separate life. All of which had little to do with Nyezhiner. She would never see him again, even though they were somehow so close . . .

When the clock struck three, Miriam was still lying fully dressed on the sofa, still listening to the footsteps in the hallway. Had David come back? If so, she would tell him only one thing: she was going, leaving the apartment and everything in it to him.

David did not come.

Toward morning, it poured. Rain lashed the windowpanes. Foghorns moaned on the river. Miriam stopped imagining she heard footsteps. She fell asleep and dreamed she was walking with Dinaleh in a magnificent garden. Tall tropical trees spread their branches above flowerbeds overflowing with rare blossoms. She had never seen such a beautiful garden. Suddenly the ground beneath them began to split apart and water gushed into the gulf. The garden broke into separate islands, each floating on its own like a colorful raft. She was on one raft, Dinaleh on another. They stretched out their hands but couldn't reach each other. The churning water separated them. She saw Dinaleh standing alone on her island as it moved farther and farther away. She cried out and struggled to wake up.

››››‹‹‹‹

Miriam found herself on the sofa, still in her clothes. A bleak, gray morning peered through the window. Everything that had happened yesterday pressed on her brain. David must have come in without her hearing him. He was probably sleeping in the bedroom. She got up from the sofa. Her dress was wrinkled, her braids tangled—she hadn't undone them since yesterday. All she wanted was to wash up, change her clothes, and not think about yesterday ever again.

She went to the bedroom. The door was open, the bed made. David wasn't there. The bed looked as lonely and forlorn as a woman deserted by her husband. The whole room looked strange. David must have spent the night in a hotel. He no longer wanted to be in the same house with her. Well, that would make the separation easier.

She washed and dressed. Dinaleh was still asleep. Miriam went to the window and looked out. The street had been washed clean by rain. There was no sign of snow, as if it had never existed. People were going to work or opening their stores. The sky looked like a face sobering up after a night on the town.

Dinaleh woke up refreshed and cheerful, and Miriam sent her off to school. After the child left it suddenly occurred to her that something might have happened to David. Should she call the drugstore? At that moment the phone rang. She picked up right away, thinking David must be calling to tell her he never wanted to see her again and wanted to settle things from a distance. But the voice on the phone was not David's. She barely recognized it. It was Nyezhiner's, sounding far away and uncertain.

"Miriam"—his voice broke—"I have a feeling something must have happened between you and David. Please! I have to know. Did I do something wrong? I didn't want to hurt you. I'm so worried about you, Miriam!"

"Don't worry," she said. "It's been a long time coming. David and I are separating."

"Oh, I've made you unhappy—as unhappy as I am. I didn't mean to cause you trouble, Miriam! I have to see you! Where can we meet? I was on my way to the shop, but I know I won't be able to work today. I'll come to you now. I have to!"

"No, no. Please don't come. I need to be alone. I need to get my thoughts in order. I'm not sure—not sure about anything."

The door opened, and David came in carrying a new suitcase in his hand. He walked past her, rigid as a soldier. She stood with the receiver in her hand and said nothing.

The voice on the telephone was insistent. "What are you unsure about, Miriam? We have to talk. If I can't see you at home, I'll wait for you by the bridge. This afternoon at one o'clock. I'll be waiting for you. Without fail."

"No, don't wait for me! I don't know anything now. I don't know when I'll see you. I can't talk anymore."

She hung up and went to the bedroom door. David was bending over a drawer, pulling out clothes. The suitcase lay open before him.

She had to speak to him right away, before he left the apartment. He had to know she had no intention of staying there. She couldn't afford the apartment or even a smaller one. Nor did she have anywhere to take their child. If she were alone, she could manage until she found a place. But their daughter needed a home, her own bed, her piano. Dinaleh would have to stay with David in the apartment for now. He could find someone to take care of her and do the housework. Later she would take the child, relieve him of the responsibility. She just needed a little time to look for a job and a home for herself and Dinaleh. She had to tell him all this. She'd thought about it all night. She even had a woman in mind: the widow who often babysat for Dinaleh when she went out. The poor woman would jump at the chance. It would be best for Dinaleh—and for her, too, because if she had to wander around with the child, she would surely end up right back here at David's feet, begging him to take her back.

Her throat was choked with tears. Don't cry in front of David, Miriam told herself. Let him think I'm tough. She went closer.

"David, I have to talk to you."

David stopped what he was doing but didn't look up. She talked to the back of his head, to his soft, boyish curls. She spoke quickly, breathlessly. She was coherent and clear. After a while, listening to her, David forgot she was talking about the two of them. She could have been reading from a script. Well, she'd always wanted to be an actress, and she had the voice for it, too.

Suddenly he kicked the suitcase away. What she was saying did concern him and her. Well, fine, let her go! Let her become whatever she wanted. Fine, he decided, he would stay here. He was glad to not have to pack his things and go live with strangers. But he'd never expected that she'd want to leave their daughter with him. Knowing her, he would never have dared ask for such a thing. He'd always let her have her way.

David felt a surge of energy. The fog pressing on his brain since yesterday began to lift. He had spent a restless night on the hard bench in the drugstore, but now he felt better. Every evening he would come home as usual and find Dinaleh awake or asleep and he'd be able to lie down and sleep in his own bed. He wanted to sleep right now, but he couldn't. The store should already be open. Let her do what she'd been wanting to do all these years. Let her!

He left the apartment with firm steps, closing the door slowly, carefully, without banging, the way one closes the door to one's own home. Miriam remained alone in the middle of the room. Alone, as if on an empty stage.

« CHAPTER 3 »

NYEZHINER FINISHED his cigarette and threw the empty pack over the railing into the water. His breath reeked of tobacco, his eyes hurt from lack of sleep, and he'd been waiting for Miriam for more than an hour. With the last drag on his cigarette it became clear to him that she wasn't coming. She must want to prove—to herself and to him—that leaving David had nothing to do with him. She'd said as much on the phone early this morning. But he'd thought it was just talk; in the end she'd show up at the appointed time because she needed him now. And here he was. But it seemed she didn't need him, or maybe she was unwilling to get involved in his complicated life. And really, what did he have to offer her? It would be different if she were deeply in love with him, but apparently she wasn't sure she was. Yesterday she'd given no sign of indecision. She sat next to him on the sofa, as trusting as a little girl. Their hands reached out and found each other and didn't let go. When it grew dark, she didn't put on the light. Both of them lost track of time and place. So why was she avoiding him now? He knew he was important to her. They wouldn't be able to avoid each other forever. But maybe between early morning and now everything had changed. He had to know. He had to see her, had to speak to her. Immediately. He decided to go to her even though she'd asked him not to.

He descended the bridge into the plaza. Cars honked, warning him to get out of the road, but he was too lost in thought to realize they were honking at him. Someone leaned out of a car window and cursed. "What are you doing, mister? Are you deaf and blind? You wanna kill yourself? Go jump off the bridge!"

For a moment he stood there, distracted and confused, while the cars swirled around him. Then he started walking again, but not as quickly. What am I doing? he asked himself. Maybe David was home and that was why Miriam didn't want him to come. What would he do if he found David at home? What would he say? "I've come to take your wife away"? No. After all, he too had a wife and children, and even though he didn't live with them, he had to provide for them. He would never be free of them, nor did he want to be. Besides, he was broke. He was no knight in shining armor, as some women might fantasize. All he could be was a thief, a cheater, stealing a woman's love.

That must be how Miriam saw him.

Burdened by these thoughts, he walked on with shoulders bowed, then straightened up and retraced his steps. He stopped at a tobacco store for a pack of cigarettes, lit up, and went to the telephone on the wall. He put in a nickel, heard a dull ring, and when the operator asked for the number, he gave Miriam's. If David answered, he'd politely ask to speak to her. That would be easier than meeting David face to face.

He waited. The ringing seemed shriller and louder than ever before. But no one answered. No one was at home, it seemed; the phone was ringing in an empty apartment. He had the feeling he was standing in that empty room, talking to the wall. He held the phone to his ear as if the ringing could communicate everything he wanted to say to Miriam. After a while he hung up. The coin sprang out with a clink. He caught the nickel in his sweating palm and went back out to the street.

There he stood, pondering where to go, what to do. Hershele

sprang to mind. How had he forgotten about him? He'd forgotten his friends, become estranged from them. He needed to see Hershele.

He walked toward his friend's home in the old part of Brooklyn.

››››‹‹‹‹

Hershele Kalish's house was dilapidated, its steps slumped like an old woman's back. Inside, though, the apartment was spotless. The curtains hung just so and the floors shone like gold. Anka took care of the household—Anka, who barely spoke and whose round young face was always smiling. When Hershele compared her to the wives of his fellow writers, he knew that his lovely, intelligent Anka came out on top. Maybe he was overstating things, but he couldn't help himself. Such exaggeration was his most charming quality. He was always courteous toward Anka, and indeed toward all women, so long as they didn't cross a certain line and annoy him. He was quite different with his male friends—gruff, even contrary with some of them, passionately devoted to others. He had bound himself to Nyezhiner from the moment they met, and his devotion knew no bounds.

Hershele Kalish was known as a writer only within the small circle of his young friends, but within that circle he loomed large right from the start. He was always at work on several long novels, all at the same time. Often enough he felt dazzled by his own carefully chosen words, each one honed and polished until it shone. Then again, he was just as often assailed by doubts about his writing talent. At those times one of his eyes would begin to twitch and he would blink, trying to stop himself from tearing up everything he'd written in his thick notebooks.

Hershele's heart fluttered nervously every time he delivered a chapter to one of his friends to publish in the new issue of the journal. Yet all of his chapters shone with refined beauty, and his fellow aesthetes loved them. He had yet to produce a complete work, but his fellow poets believed in his talent and didn't mind. He didn't really belong with the prose writers of *Di Yunge*. Both his writing and his excitable temperament were more in tune with the poets. Barely thirty years old, he sported a stumpy little beard, and his dark eyes smoldered with writerly passion, as if he were possessed. His hands were broad with flat fingers. His first rough handshake brought a smile to Nyezhiner's face, and their friendship was sealed.

Although Hershele had the look of an absent-minded artist, he was in fact a practical young man with a keen business sense, no doubt inherited from the generations of merchants in his family. In addition to writing he was involved in the printing side of the literary world. He planned to establish a big Yiddish publishing house and was always on the brink of bankruptcy.

Hershele and Nyezhiner often strolled through the streets of Brooklyn beyond the Jewish neighborhoods. Nyezhiner would talk while Hershele listened. Nyezhiner spoke with urgent enthusiasm, all in a rush. A new thought popped into his head every minute. His words would flare up, then fade away, as his poetic moods waxed and waned. And then all at once he would stop talking abstractly and begin speaking quite personally, even ruthlessly, about himself.

Hershele loved their talks. Nyezhiner often said what Hershele was thinking but wasn't brave enough to express out loud. Later in their friendship, though, he was able to say affectionately: "Only a lyrical poet can cut so cruelly with his words."

And Nyezhiner's green eyes would laugh.

When Hershele came home after a walk with Nyezhiner, he would sit at his desk all night. He wrote well then. Anka once said Nyezhiner tuned his writerly strings. She said this with a broad smile on her round face. It was impossible to tell whether the thought pleased her or bothered her.

››››‹‹‹‹

Now Nyezhiner walked without seeing the streets or the houses, yet he stopped right at Hershele's house, in front of the sagging steps. He knocked on the door and went in without waiting for an answer. Anka greeted him with her usual smile, showing her small, even teeth.

"I'm glad you're here," she said. "Hershele has been pining for you like a lover. Even I was beginning to worry."

Hershele was indeed looking forward to Nyezhiner's arrival. But he also felt insulted. What kind of friend would forget about him like this? Here they were planning to launch a new journal and his friend was nowhere to be found. No doubt off chasing some skirt again. Let him just show up—he'd tell him off to his face! This time they would quarrel, he knew it.

But when Hershele came out to greet his friend and saw Nyezhiner's face, he didn't say a word. He could tell something was very wrong.

They went into the room Anka called his study, which contained his desk, a narrow couch, an old rocking chair, a bookshelf, and an old-fashioned clock that chimed the hours. All the furniture was second-hand, but Anka had made everything clean and tidy.

Hershele perched on the desk, his eyes blinking nervously as Nyezhiner settled himself in the rocking chair, crossed his ankles, lit a cigarette, and said nothing.

Finally he spoke four words: "My life is over."

"Over? But why?"

Nyezhiner pretended not to hear Hershele's ironic tone. He knew his friend was annoyed with him, and after all, he had a right to be. The sarcasm didn't bother him. Hershele was letting him know he felt wronged. That didn't threaten their friendship. He could tell Hershele things he couldn't say to anyone else, even now, when Hershele was in a bad mood.

"It looks as if Miriam is separating from her husband," Nyezhiner said, as if talking to himself. "I should have known I'd ruin her life! She says it's not my fault—it's not because of me. But now she's avoiding me. Do you see?" (Strangely, the two friends spoke to each other using the formal Yiddish "you.")

"So you've got yourself a new scandal!" Hershele thought. "A new mess!"

Hershele wanted to curse at his friend but couldn't bring himself to do so. He had too much regard for the man bent over in the chair before him. He just blinked and waited for Nyezhiner to go on.

Nyezhiner had nothing more to say. His green eyes seemed clouded over with gray. He stared straight ahead, smoking, his narrow shoulders stooped.

"I don't see why you're so depressed," Hershele said.

Nyezhiner gave him a sharp look.

"I thought," said Hershele slowly, "that you wouldn't fall in love again after what happened last time, with Lily."

"Hershele, you're a fool," said Nyezhiner, also slowly. "You don't understand a thing."

"No, I do understand," Hershele said. "I understand perfectly well that *you* don't understand a thing about love. I'm the one who knows it's all rubbish."

"Hershele, stop playing the cynic."

"Who's playing? I'm serious. I saw what happened to you before. Apparently you didn't learn a thing from that experience."

"But Hershele, not every experience is the same."

"Oh? So this time you're really in love?"

With that, Hershele sprang off the desk. Nyezhiner smiled wryly as Hershele started pacing back and forth, clasping and unclasping his large hands and cracking his knuckles one after the other. Now and then Hershele glanced over at Nyezhiner in his chair, and something tore at his heart. All of a sudden he stopped in front of his friend.

"Listen to me. This woman Miriam isn't going to let you go. She's toying with you. You may think I don't know women, but you're wrong. I know them better than you do. A poet, even the best poet, can afford to be naïve, even a fool. It doesn't hurt him. A prose writer like me has to have common sense as well as talent. Do you understand? A woman doesn't leave one man until she's found another. If she's really left her husband, then she's got her eye on you, and she'll hunt you down until she gets you. Just wait. You'll see I know what I'm talking about."

Nyezhiner looked up with a smile. He got a kick out of Hershele's impertinence, his boasts about how well he knew women. Still, it was possible there was a hidden truth in Hershele's words, even if Miriam herself didn't know it yet.

"I won't let you leave here without having something to eat," Hershele said calmly. "And then we have to talk about the journal. I looked for you in the café yesterday. I sat there with Yankev Shor and waited in case you came. I wanted to remind you—maybe you've forgotten—that the young 'pipsqueaks' are coming over today. Of course! You did forget. Also, the check came, the honorarium for your ballad. I took it over to Chana, as you requested."

Hershele wanted to add that it wouldn't have hurt for Nyezhiner to deliver the check to his wife himself. But he saw straightaway that the smile had disappeared from Nyezhiner's face. He looked tense and stubborn. Hershele said nothing more.

Nyezhiner's stiff demeanor softened. "I know I'm taking advantage of you," he said. "But what can I do? I know you're bailing me out by going over there. I've burdened you with my problems. Oh, I'm useless." He bowed his head.

"Now, now," said Hershele. "Still, maybe you really should go yourself. If I can allow myself to say so."

"What do you know?" said Nyezhiner, glaring at him. "You don't understand that Chana can't stand it when I go over to see the children. If I go, I'm supposed to stay with her, be her husband as God commanded. Like before. Do you understand? But I can't do it anymore. I can't. It's over."

Hershele stroked his beard. The truth was he had been hoping that one of these days Nyezhiner would leave "the other woman" and go back to Chana, tired and disappointed, and be a husband to his wife and a father to his children. But now, like a demon, Miriam had appeared.

There was a knock at the door, and Anka came in with her usual broad smile, excusing herself and saying the food was getting cold.

When Anka had cleared the dishes, Nyezhiner stayed sitting at the table, overcome by sleepiness. His head drooped, and he surrendered to the weariness. It was still early in the evening, and their colleagues were due in an hour or two. Hershele, who had hoped to talk to Nyezhiner about the new journal before the others came, didn't have the heart to disturb his friend.

"Maybe you want to lie down for a bit on the couch in Hershele's room?" asked Anka. "You don't look quite right."

"Thank you, Anka. I'm just tired. I didn't sleep much last night. I'll go take a little nap."

« CHAPTER 4 »

NYEZHINER STRETCHED out on the hard couch in Hershele's study, and before he was even asleep he was entangled in a web of dreams about what had occurred that day: waiting for Miriam on the bridge, setting out for her house, and walking into the middle of traffic in the plaza. But in the web of his dream, Miriam was standing across the plaza, and she could see everything. She could see him standing like a dimwit, unable to move, with the traffic roaring around him. Miriam left, and he wanted to yell to her to wait. He'd go with her. But he couldn't speak. His voice was gone, somewhere deep inside him. He was frightened. He had to find his voice. He had to scream. He fought with all his strength. Then he realized he was asleep. Sleep held him in a tight grip and wanted to strangle his voice. But he wouldn't let it! He would cheat sleep. He cried out and awoke.

It was dark. At first he didn't know where he was. But then he heard voices in the other room, the familiar voices of his friends, and he knew he had to get up and go to them. He wanted to close his eyes again, but he forced himself up, shivering, and opened the door. He could hear his friends' voices and see the clouds of their cigarette smoke.

"There he is! Nyezhiner!" Yankev Shor said in a sing-song

voice, coming toward him with a smile and hands outstretched. "I haven't seen you in ages."

"All right, can we finally begin?" said Hersh Berman impatiently, as if he had only been waiting for Nyezhiner in order to open the meeting.

Nyezhiner yawned, stretched, and shivered some more, even though it was warm in the packed room.

Shor didn't take his eyes off Nyezhiner. He was a bit jealous of Nyezhiner's nomadic life, his restlessness. That was how a poet should live! That was how one wrote meaningful poems. A poet had to get off the beaten track, Shor said to himself. He smiled, but his eyes betrayed his sadness.

Hersh Berman came over and placed a firm hand on Nyezhiner's shoulder. "I have to talk to you, but not now. Later." And with that he went back to the table and called the meeting to order.

The room was full, and cigarette smoke rose to the ceiling.

Itche Lichtenstein had chosen a spot in the corner of the room, a cigarette dangling from his full lips. He was no longer the slim boy he had once been. His thighs had thickened, his corpulent chest looked puffy, as if yeast had caused it to rise, and his golden hair had lost its luster. But his carefully tousled curls still cascaded down his forehead into his violet-blue eyes.

Itchele pretended not to notice Nyezhiner's entrance. He took a small book with tiny print out of his vest pocket and began to sway as if in prayer. Itchele wasn't jealous of anyone. Nyezhiner's talent moved him. The freshness and originality of his words intrigued and excited him. But he wouldn't talk about it the way others did. When the rest were enthusiastic he was calm. He might roll his eyes and whisper to Shor or Hershele that Nyezhiner was flying too high with his muse. And Nyezhiner's great romances just made him sigh. He considered himself above such things, and so did his friends.

Itchele's wisdom was more felt than heard. He spoke little, sometimes with a stutter. His poems also often stuttered. Still, his friends regarded him as a significant poet and a leading voice, Nyezhiner even more than the others. He knew words didn't come as easily to Itchele as they did to him, although Itchele never said as much. He knew how Itchele struggled to find the right words, how meticulous he was, how his lips caressed every word, how he loved the Yiddish language so much that it pained him.

Itchele and Nyezhiner had a push-and-pull relationship. They were drawn to each other's talents, but those talents were so different that sometimes they couldn't stand each other. Sometimes one of them threw out a word as sharp as a sword and they faced off as if in a duel. But in the end they never drew their weapons.

There were other talented writers in the room, but none with the power to lead. And there were also beginners who sat in silent rapture looking up to the others.

Itchele Lichtenstein closed his book with its tiny print, raised his violet eyes to the ceiling, furrowed his pale brow, and said, "Well?"

The meeting had begun.

Hersh Berman was chair. His energy and ambition outstripped everyone else's, and that made him the group's leader. He had already published several novels and was always working on another. He took on the hardest work, including playing a major role in producing the journals. Nonetheless, perhaps precisely because of his energy and ambition, he remained a stranger to most of his colleagues. Hershele Kalish couldn't stand him. He even belittled Berman's talent. He couldn't bear how Berman was able to take on so much work, carry out everything efficiently, and get it all done on time. Hershele himself was also enterprising. He understood and liked the business side of books and journals, but he couldn't do a single thing exactly right or on time. This didn't really trouble him. In fact, he believed his lack of precision and his frequent business failures were an indication that precision and success didn't necessarily align with talent. He had quite a lot to say about Hersh Berman. Quite a lot. But not now. Now his eye twitched nervously as he observed the self-assurance with which Berman chaired the meeting.

The room was thick with smoke, talk, commotion. But when Itchele Lichtenstein spoke up from his corner, everyone fell silent. In the silence, Itchele slowly and calmly measured out his words. Few as they were, each one carried the weight of a thousand years of experience. No one disagreed with him. Despite the occasional stammer, his words were so true, so full of tact and wisdom.

Nyezhiner smiled and raised his hand to signal his agreement with Itchele. Hershele Kalish grew calm, even happy. Now he knew that both Itchele and Nyezhiner would be involved in the new journal, and no one mattered to him as much as those two.

Anka brought in tea and cookies. She had been waiting for Hershele to give a sign that the formal part of the evening was over. Everyone started speaking at once, interrupting, arguing noisily, as in every big family. Soon they'd read out their latest poems, look into one another's eyes, wait for a compliment, a good word, the only reward that mattered.

Yankev Shor sought out Itchele, who was standing in a corner with a glass of tea. Shor seized him by the lapel and recited some poems in a Hasidic sing-song—not his own poems but the work of Elsa Lasker-Shuler. And while Itchele stood listening, half-curiously and half-impatiently, Hersh Berman made his way across the crowded room to Nyezhiner. Before he even got close, his protruding jaw already seemed to demand something.

"What's happening with the poem? Have you finished it?" Berman asked unceremoniously.

"Well . . . almost. I still need to work on a few little—"

"Then when? We need to go to press. You're making us delay the whole issue."

"So delay it. Or don't delay it. Does the whole world depend on me?"

"Listen to me," said Berman, changing his tone. "Go into the other room, away from all this noise, and you'll finish the poem in no time. Give it to me, and I'll take it straight to the printer."

"Stop!" Nyezhiner cried. He forced himself to smile. "Why now, when there's so much going on, so much fun?"

"Listen to me," Berman repeated. He put his hands forcefully on Nyezhiner's shoulders. "Do it now."

"Leave me alone!" said Nyezhiner with a frown. "Can't you loosen up for even one minute? Yes, literature! But—"

While he was talking, the door opened and a young woman came in. She wore a tight jacket and a Persian lamb hat pulled down low, and she held her hands in a muff. She looked around a bit bewildered.

Anka came over to her with a smile. "You're not lost, Julia. Do come in!"

Julia giggled. "I was walking by and all your lights were on, so I thought I'd stop by. I haven't seen you in so long. But maybe I'm in the way?"

"Of course not! Why would you think that?" said Hershele, suddenly at her side. "Far from it! You're most welcome. You came at just the right time. I'll introduce you to everyone. Some you already know."

He took Julia's arm. "This is Julia Polonski, my relative. She's a nurse in the hospital near here. Quite the pretty little woman, yes?"

Julia gave another little laugh.

Some around the table stood up, others just nodded. Yankev Shor narrowed his eyes and stared intently at Julia's dark, thin face.

Anka brought her some tea. "Here you are."

Hershele asked if she'd had any letters from Eliezer, her husband, who had gone with a group of other young Americans to serve in the Jewish Legion in Palestine. "What does he say?"

He was doing well, Julia said with another breathless giggle, and he was finding it very interesting. To Anka she had confided more about what he'd said in his most recent letter. He'd met up with Elisheva. "Remember her—the woman he was once engaged to?" Eliezer wrote that she had divorced her husband and was prettier than ever, her face free of pimples.

Julia laughed, speaking loudly, like a child trying to attract attention.

All the literary conversations had broken off when Julia came in, and now they were slow to resume.

Nyezhiner realized that Berman had disappeared. Now, as always, he regretted having hurt him, having pushed him away. He looked around and saw him sitting alone, his strong chin leaning on his big hands, like Rodin's *The Thinker*. Itchele had once dubbed Berman "The Young Thinker." Nyezhiner smiled. How appropriate! His earlier anger toward Berman faded. Calmly, Nyezhiner thought: all right, if Berman wants to build his own career so quickly, with the *hury-op* tempo of America, then let him. Who's to stop him? He wants to lead? Fine! But what does he want with me? Why does he have to grab my poems before I've even written them, in such a panic, as if there were a competition? I've told him off so many times, but nothing works. He's determined to be my conscience.

Nyezhiner remembered an evening here at Hershele's home. A few friends had gathered to talk about a literary matter, and afterward he and Itchele sat down to a game of chess. Berman looked at him as if to say, "Chess? You lazy bum! Why aren't you working on the poems you were whispering in my ear yesterday?"

Well, sure, he knew he wasn't a great chess player. Itchele could easily get the better of him. But he liked playing every kind of game, even cards. That's exactly when poems would come into his head, to the detriment of his strategy on the board. Sometimes he would forget these poems, sometimes not. But he needed to play. Berman didn't understand. That evening Berman hadn't left his side. He saw that Nyezhiner was losing. "Stop playing!" he nagged. "Go home and write down the last lines before you forget."

Nyezhiner had angrily shooed him away, blown up at him, and

Berman had left, insulted. Then he'd quit the game, because inside him something had begun to cry. It was Berman crying over his—Nyezhiner's—impractical nature.

That night he did write down the children's prose poem he'd begun whispering to Berman. He could see Berman's resentful shadow looking over his shoulder the whole time he was writing. Well, of course Berman was devoted to him, of course he worried about him. Poor Berman! He worried over the fate of literature itself. The truth was he couldn't free himself from Berman, and apparently he didn't want to.

Now Nyezhiner went over to where Berman was sitting, chin propped in his hand, thinking. He stood before him with an apologetic smile.

"You see, you've won again. I'm going to Hershele's room to finish the poem, and rest assured it's all because of you. Hershele will take it to the printer."

And Nyezhiner was off.

Berman was so moved that tears came to his eyes. He wanted to call out after his friend: "I like you just the way you are! I love you for your talent, your exuberant words, your boyish charm—and maybe for your impracticality, too."

Now Berman took his leave from the gathering. His sweet young wife was waiting for him at home, along with the attic room full of his novel in progress, which he loved not less than his wife.

It was one in the morning when Hershele ushered his guests out. They went quietly down the stairs so as not to wake the neighbors. In the dark corridor, Yankev Shor held Julia's arm. Out on the street, they stood apart from the others. She wanted to laugh aloud at what Shor was saying, but she hid her mouth behind her hand because the unlit windows of the entire street seemed to whisper: "Ssh, people are sleeping." Shor took her arm companionably to walk her home.

Around two, Nyezhiner crept out of Hershele's study. On the desk he'd left his finished poem along with a note for Hershele telling him to take it to the printer.

Hershele suddenly appeared in his bathrobe.

"Where are you going in the middle of the night, in this cold? You can sleep here. I'll make up a bed for you on the sofa."

Nyezhiner declined with a wave of the hand, and Hershele went looking for his friend's hat and coat. In the dim room both of their shadows looked enormous, but one was a little bigger. The bigger one crept out of the house.

Outside, Nyezhiner pulled up his collar against the wind and strode through the nighttime streets of Brooklyn to his furnished room. His thoughts returned to Miriam. Maybe she'd been there looking for him. Maybe she'd left a note. It was possible.

« CHAPTER 5 »

1. SUITCASE IN HAND, Miriam arrived at her brother Moyshe's apartment as if returning home after a long trip. Her mother was at Moyshe's, and everything was the same as it had been years ago. Here was Moyshe's wife, Freydl, the same Freydl with her round, ruddy face, her big-boned body, and her anxious heart. Freydl was staunchly devoted to Moyshe's family because she had none of her own here in America. That had been the case when she married, and so it was today.

Because Moyshe was the oldest of Chaye Soreh's three children, he'd tried after their father died to step into his shoes and provide for the family, both in their poor home in the shtetl and later in the big city in Ukraine. He looked out for his two sisters, Malke and Miriam. Miriam, the younger one, was wild and refused to mind him. Moyshe scolded her when she misbehaved. He would draw himself up to his full height and stand there tall and handsome, twirling his new brown mustache and barely suppressing a smile because he knew the role of patriarch didn't suit him at all. Throughout her childhood, Miriam loved him deeply but never obeyed him.

Now Miriam came in with her suitcase and looked at Moyshe's face as he stood there the way he used to, twirling his mustache, which had sprouted a bit of gray. She remembered how he would scold her when she misbehaved as a child. He'd better not try to take on the role of father now. She was too tired to muster an ounce of patience for his speeches, no matter how much she still loved his smile.

Her mother was sitting in her old chair. Her arms were folded and her face was soft, subdued, wrinkled with worry. Seeing her, Miriam felt she still belonged in this home that she'd left seven years ago to marry David. Nonetheless, she probably wouldn't have come here if she'd had an alternative.

When she left David, he hadn't even asked if she needed money. Not that she would have taken it. In all their years together she'd held herself apart from everything of his, even the household goods and furniture. Everything in the house, she felt, belonged to him. He'd worked for it. She owned nothing of her own, not even a piece of jewelry. It wasn't that David was stingy. On the contrary, he often wanted to buy her things, but she wouldn't let him. Well, now she had to make her own way. She just had to overcome this first difficult period, find a job and get settled, and then she would bring Dinaleh to live with her.

Here at Moyshe's they'd been expecting her. They knew. Things happen between couples, Moyshe thought. In time, things would go back to normal, but meanwhile he'd need to keep an eye on her. It was better for her to be here than anywhere else. Freydl looked worried as she prepared a bed for Miriam in the parlor. She had no idea what Miriam was up to, but she couldn't turn her away. She had always respected Miriam, admired her even though she'd never understood her. One thing was clear: Miriam was different from everyone else in the family. The look in her eyes, her speech, everything about her was different. Often she'd wanted to be like Miriam, just as she sometimes wanted to be the heroine of one of the novels she read in the newspaper. But Freydl knew she would always be Freydl and never the heroine of a novel, because she didn't really know how. She had a kind of respect for Miriam that she felt for no one else—except for her mother-in-law, of course. She could never deny Miriam anything, and she knew that

Moyshe, for all his supposed strictness, couldn't either.

Miriam said nothing to anyone and went straight to the parlor. She hoped no one would ask her anything so she wouldn't have to explain herself. The truth was she didn't know what to say. She felt strangely alienated from herself and from the feelings and thoughts she'd had yesterday. While she was packing, there were moments when she forgot how everything had happened. Why was she separating from David? She'd done everything as though someone were making her, as though the whole thing had been dreamed up years before, had become a secret obsession, and now finally she had to go through with it. It was true that for years both she and David had known they were partly strangers to one another and the day would come when they would become complete strangers. Perhaps they had been waiting for that day. In any case, the day was here, and she mustn't lose heart simply because it scared her to think of becoming free and leaving her child with him. She was already having moments of weakness, of wanting to go back to what was before . . . to her child . . . to forget entirely about herself . . . But, no, she dared not give in. She would regret it later. It had already happened once before. She'd left David, then gone back to him, and immediately wanted to leave again. Now she had to be firm. She could feel a hidden strength protecting her from temptation, helping her to be firm, to hold out against her own weakness.

Here at Moyshe's, the family sat as if in mourning. Most evenings Moyshe would come home tired from his day in the shop and take a nap. Not today. Today he was alert. More than anyone else, Miriam wanted to avoid Moyshe's lovely face and smile.

She stretched out on the worn sofa in the parlor, staring at the old pieces of furniture as if they were old friends who had aged and become strangers during the passing years. She could feel the poverty, the stagnation, of this place that had once been her home, and now it seemed very, very strange. Why had she come here with her problems, which seemed so foreign to her family? What would become of her now?

Tears began to roll down her cheeks. And suddenly Moyshe was in the room, standing a little apart, looking at her with his soft, brown eyes and pulling at his mustache, just like when she was a child. "Why are you crying?" he said after a moment. "After all, you're doing what you want. You've always done what you wanted. So why are you crying?"

"Moyshe, come here," Freydl called anxiously to her husband.

In the other room, Chaye Soreh looked at Freydl affectionately. She sighed and dropped her veiny hands into her lap. Every wrinkle on her face reflected her thoughts. "You see? A woman should never depend on a man. Or maybe that's just true in our family."

Chaye Soreh remembered her own mother, may she rest in peace, also named Miriam. She'd run away from her first husband because he was so undependable. He was actually rather well-to-do, but he was a common furrier who smelled of sheepskin. His hands were as hard as leather when he touched her, making her blood run cold. Finally, when he was away peddling his sheepskins and hats in the villages, she packed her clothes in a bundle and ran away, back to her widowed mother in town. Everyone had a fit. The rabbi himself ordered her to go back to her husband the furrier. But she didn't listen, and the unfortunate furrier soon died of cholera in the village. Then she married her second husband, a young widower with five little children. She was healthy and young and soon began having children of her own, and with her first child still at her breast she went to the marketplace, put up a stand, and started selling dry goods to Jewish and non-Jewish women alike—bargaining, then traveling, because her husband, Chaye Soreh's father, may he rest in peace, was studying Talmud. He had delicate, lovely hands that inscribed the letters of the Bible onto parchment and earned next to nothing, while she, the mother, walked on tiptoe around him, suffered all her life, and never complained. Knowing her mother's experience, what could Chaye Soreh say to her daughter, her modern Miriam? If Miriam was, God forbid, doing something wrong, she, Chaye Soreh, couldn't be the one to judge her. She did not know better than He who governed the world, who knew its hidden ways and decided everyone's fate. Maybe what was happening to Miriam was meant to be.

So Chaye Soreh rubbed her mouth with her old, dry hand and said nothing. What was there to say?

2. Miriam fell asleep on the sofa, and when she awoke it was a new day and she felt like a new person. The girlish joy of being free, of belonging to no one, returned. It was a rare, pure sensation that made her feel as if she were swimming alone in a clear stream flowing just for her. This was the free girlhood she'd been longing for. But no, she hadn't longed only for that. She also longed for something else, something that had yet to be revealed, a secret something that was waiting for her. She wanted to be free to discover that secret.

So far, however, Miriam's days were sad and full of anxiety. Every evening she went to see Dinaleh and every evening she felt afraid until the moment she saw the child she'd left to be cared for by others. David knew she came every day, and he didn't mind. Let her come if she wanted to. Dinaleh need not suffer just because he had been wronged. He was not bitter toward Miriam. On the contrary, he still felt tender and devoted to her. It was Mrs. Stein who was bitter. She was the woman who looked after Dinaleh, a lonely middle-aged widow who suffered from gallstones and was a frequent customer in David's pharmacy. Mrs. Stein was happy to care for Dinaleh and the household. It was easy work, and Dinaleh was at school most of the day. But what bothered her—what she couldn't stand—was when Miriam came flying in every evening to clasp the child to herself, look into her eyes, examine her head, her ears. She even wanted to feed Dinaleh herself, bathe her, put her to bed. And she didn't leave until the child fell asleep.

While Miriam fussed over Dinaleh, Mrs. Stein would sit in the kitchen reading a serialized novel in the newspaper. When she finished that day's episode and had to wait for the next one, her thoughts would wander to Miriam. For the life of her, she couldn't understand this woman. How do you leave such a home, a child, and run away? Rumor had it she had a lover. In the past, whenever she'd seen Miriam in the drugstore, she'd thought something was not quite right between her and the pharmacist. But hoping for a woman worthy of him was like waiting for the coming of the Messiah. What were the odds these days that a well-established man could find a decent woman? A hundred to one!

Mrs. Stein sighed over her own fate. God only knew who would receive and who would not. She thrust out her double chin and said nothing.

Miriam was pleased with Mrs. Stein's silence, double chin and all. She didn't even mind her taking David's side. Her own family had done so; let Mrs. Stein do the same. She was better for Dinaleh than an indifferent stranger.

Evening after evening, it was almost nine o'clock before Dinaleh fell asleep listening to the story Miriam whispered to her. Miriam would kiss her sleeping child, take her coat, and say good night to Mrs. Stein. Sometimes Mrs. Stein muttered an answer, sometimes she didn't, and Miriam comforted herself with the thought that Dinaleh wouldn't be staying there beyond the winter. But why did the days drag by so slowly? It seemed like a long time since she'd left home and started coming to Dinaleh every evening. But actually it had been less than two weeks.

3. Out in the cold, Miriam suddenly felt hungry. She'd had no appetite at lunchtime and hadn't eaten since morning, when her mother served her breakfast. Her mother was worried that she'd grown thin. "Miriam dear," she said, looking at her daughter's slim shoulders, "if your soul hadn't gotten caught on one of your little bones, it would have flown away." Her mother understood every-

thing without asking. A hot meal was always waiting when Miriam came in, whether early or late. Meanwhile, Moyshe twirled his mustache and said nothing. She thought he might be getting ready to have a word with her, but he couldn't because Ada came over almost every evening to spend time with her in the parlor, and by the time she left Moyshe was already asleep.

Tonight Miriam wanted to be alone, without Ada. She wanted to stretch out on the sofa and fall asleep. She was very tired, having spent the whole day finding a job. She could have started work today, but she'd made up some excuse and promised to come tomorrow. The factory scared her. Young people sat glued to their machines, hurrying to keep pace. The machines made a huge racket, but the workers seemed oblivious to the noise and perhaps also to the fact that outside there was a sun, a sky, trees. They were accustomed to the dim, narrow streets that ran between the tall factory buildings on Broadway and the warehouses along the Hudson. It was strange to think that by the time she was fifteen she herself was already used to the sweatshop and the damp, narrow streets of the workers' quarter. She'd been surrounded by grayness and poverty, but at the time she hadn't seen it. Now, after seven years with David, the comfortable apartment, summers in the countryside, free time to stroll in the park, concerts, museums, books—now she saw with different eyes.

Well, today was a bad day, Miriam said to herself. Even Dinaleh had looked at her with sad circles under her eyes. My God, Miriam cried, let it not come to what Moyshe was expecting, and maybe David, too. Everyone was waiting for her to fail and go back to her previous life. To David.

The cold made her shiver as she walked toward Moyshe's. The ground under her feet was covered with a layer of frost that she could feel through the thin soles of her shoes. She remembered that she had several pairs of high-laced boots. Why hadn't she worn them today? Because their heels were too high for all the walking she'd had to do. Suddenly she recalled the sentence "You're wearing deerskin shoes." And once again she realized Nyezhiner was on her mind even when she wasn't thinking about him. And even though she'd told herself again and again that it wasn't because of him that she'd separated from David, somewhere deep inside she knew she wouldn't have had the courage to leave, with all the difficulties entailed, if Nyezhiner hadn't appeared in her life. Yes, she was full of negative feelings and jealousy when it came to him and his past life, but she also knew that he stood between her and David, protecting her from temptation, barring her from giving in to weakness and going back to all she had left behind. She was well aware, too, that today or tomorrow he would show up again. Every evening when she left Dinaleh and went back to Moyshe's she imagined him waiting on every corner, watching her every step. Often, she hurried along as if to avoid him—and still she looked for him.

Hurrying distractedly, Miriam almost passed by Moyshe's house. But suddenly, as if someone had called out to her, she stopped and looked up—and there, by the steps to the building, as if rooted to the spot, stood Nyezhiner. She was not one bit surprised. She smiled.

"What are you doing here?"

"No one runs away from me. If I want to find you, I will." And he stuck out his chin stubbornly.

"How did you know where I was?"

"I'm like a bloodhound—I sniff out everything." He took her hand and held it fast.

Suddenly, all her previous thoughts were wiped away. His stubborn words, and how tightly he held her hand, as though he were afraid she would tear it away and flee—all this surprised her and made her happy. She laughed—a burst of laughter that erupted on its own, beyond her control.

A thought entered Nyezhiner's head: if only Hershele could hear her laugh! He grasped her hand even tighter.

"My hand," she whimpered. "I'm weak. I've hardly eaten anything today."

"Let's go, then," he said, starting off without letting go of her hand. Miriam practically had to run to keep up with his long, quick steps.

Now her hand lay in the crook of his arm, tightly pressed to his ribs. She could feel the warmth of his body through his light coat. All thoughts had fled from her head; in her heart, all objections had dissolved. No words passed their lips. They joined the crowd at the bridge plaza and soon found themselves on Broadway, in the dim recess below the El. Here he bent down to her, almost hiding her body with his, and amid the clatter of the El, among the hurrying crowd, they kissed for the first time. Yes, the first time. Miriam closed her eyes as if she were no longer in possession of her own free will, no longer wanted to have any say in her own life. Her heart was full of sadness mixed with joy. Nyezhiner felt her salty tears on his lips. He kissed her eyelids, then caught himself abruptly.

"Little one, maybe you're crying because you're hungry?" he said, addressing her for the first time with the informal *you*. "Here's the restaurant."

Red lobsters, glistening fish, and juicy steaks, the small restaurant's specialties, were displayed on crushed ice in the window. Because of the late hour, it was nearly empty inside, quiet and dimly lit. White napkins lay peacefully on the tables.

They chose a table in a secluded corner and sat looking into each other's eyes. Miriam's eyes grew larger and more trusting, and Nyezhiner's shone as green and fresh as grass.

The waiter came, and Nyezhiner ordered a steak for Miriam and fried oysters for himself.

"Well, little one, do you want to know how I found your new address?" He grinned. "I got it from Ada. I hung around your house for many days to no avail. You were hiding. You wanted me to chase you like a young boy. Fine." And his hands crept across the table and clasped her fingers. "Well, now you're doomed. I've found you." And he gripped her fingers tighter. For a moment, his chin stuck out stubbornly, and his front teeth gleamed through parted lips.

"You're right," Miriam said with a smile both shrewd and submissive. "I'm doomed."

The food was still sizzling when the waiter brought it to the table. But there it remained, forgotten, growing cold. They sat at the table, hand in hand, their fingers woven together, looking into each other's eyes.

"Oh!" Nyezhiner said suddenly. "I just remembered you're starving!" He let go of her hands.

But Miriam was no longer hungry. She couldn't touch her food. Nyezhiner tore off a bit of a roll and brought it to her mouth, and she touched his fingers with her lips.

They ate mechanically, as if embarrassed to be eating, taking no pleasure in the food. Then they stood up and left the restaurant.

They walked silently, arm in arm. Miriam didn't ask where they were going, as if she knew without words. The cold bored into them, the ice crunched underfoot. The dim streets, poorly lit, stretched out straight before them and disappeared into the night. The houses on both sides of the street seemed poured from the same mold, all alike, all silent. Here and there a sign swayed in the wind. Nyezhiner stopped in front of one silent old house, a three-story brownstone squeezed between two others. Miriam looked up at a sign: "Furnished Rooms."

"This is where I live," said Nyezhiner furrowing his brow.

Miriam shivered. Her teeth were chattering. She waited for him to unlock the outer door. As quiet as thieves, they climbed the carpeted stairs, dusty and trodden by untold numbers.

Nyezhiner unlocked the door to his room and Miriam went in. He pressed a button on the wall and a small overhead lamp spread a dim yellow light. Miriam looked around. Yes, the room was exactly as he had described: there was a narrow bed with an iron frame, a tall dresser, a chair, a window looking out on a courtyard, an inscrutable silence.

The room was icy, as if it had never been heated. They wrapped themselves around each other. Miriam reached her cold fingers inside his loose collar and hid them there. He lifted her up, cradled her in his arms. She felt her braids slide down over her shoulders, heard her shoes fall to the floor. The ceiling lamp was dark, and she squeezed her eyes shut. Let him hold her closer, carry her away, far, far away to the end of the earth, to the end of her very self.

« CHAPTER 6 »

EVERY EVENING, Miriam rushed from the shop to see Dinaleh. By design, David was never home then, and Mrs. Stein went off with her newspaper while Miriam tended to her child. She bathed her, combed her hair, looked over her clothes to make sure they were in order, and took care of her until bedtime and the story that Dinaleh waited for impatiently. Miriam thought up the story on the spot, sitting at her daughter's bedside. Sometimes it happened that she would fall silent, as if she were lost in thought or had forgotten the thread of the story. Then Dinaleh, half asleep, would tell her what had to happen next. When Dinaleh fell asleep Miriam hurried off, because Nyezhiner would be waiting for her.

Nyezhiner waited on the corner opposite Moyshe's house. From afar, he saw her hurrying with her quick steps, and his shadow unfolded as he came to meet her. He took her hand, kissed her fingers, looked into her eyes.

"You look pale, little one. Hard work? You must be hungry. Still, the world is a lovely place. You'll soon see!" And he spread his hand in the air as if to wipe away the hard gray reality.

Miriam forgot how tired and hungry she was. His waiting patiently for her to come back from Dinaleh erased all the difficulties of the day. She took his arm and her steps quickened and they went to eat in their restaurant, where they were nearly alone. They held hands across the tablecloth and gazed into each other's eyes. He talked childish nonsense to her and often he whispered his poems.

Miriam loved his sing-song whispering, the way his head rocked back and forth, the faces he made. Still, she knew that now, after a day's work in the factory, her fingers pricked by the needle and her weary shoulders bowed—now the poems he whispered didn't touch her the way they had in the days when she wasn't so tired. While he held her hand and whispered so rhythmically and softly, Miriam thought about looking for a different job, away from the factory. She was afraid of the weariness that dulled her senses. She saw this dullness in the faces of the overburdened workers around her all day. And Nyezhiner? Why hadn't the long years at the machine made him dull? He was an exception, a miracle the likes of which one didn't often find.

They met outside Moyshe's house nearly every night. Where could one go on long winter evenings? He was not allowed to bring women to his furnished room. Landladies were strict about that, though one could creep in secretly. Heart pounding, Miriam had done this more than once. What else? Get a room together? But the winter would soon pass, and she would be going to the mountains with Dinaleh. So why take such a step, especially since she was not at all certain in her heart that this was what she wanted? She didn't yet know how strong her feelings were. It might be that everything between them would end as all his previous loves had ended. A part of her was expecting just that. She often thought about his wife and children, about his earlier affairs, and that made her withdraw.

Because they had no home, they often went to the movies. There, in the dark, like all the other couples, they held hands, embraced, and ignored the screen. But sometimes the movie caught their attention. The silent heroes of the drama enacted their pain, their love, their hatred. Often they left the movies with heads bowed by the heavy weight of life, ready to go their separate ways.

By the end of winter, Miriam cheered up. Now the factory's busy season was over, and soon she would be spending all summer in the mountains with Dinaleh. She had spoken with David, and he'd offered to cover all of Dinaleh's expenses through the summer and beyond, when she would return to the city and Dinaleh would stay with her. He seemed to have lost interest in the household. He was seldom home, and Mrs. Stein had frequent gallstone attacks. He couldn't wait for the day when Miriam would take Dinaleh.

Quickly and animatedly, Miriam told Nyezhiner all this when they met. He said nothing. Her liveliness made him feel sad. She was ready to go away with her child for the whole summer. But what about him? Wasn't she thinking about him at all? He was up in the air, neither here nor there. She could have taken an apartment already, and that would have given him a place, a home. But the child was more important. Dinaleh wasn't used to spending the summer in the city, nor was she. So he would have to spend all summer alone in his stuffy room.

"I don't want to go to our usual restaurant tonight," said Miriam playfully. "I want to be among a lot of people."

He glanced at her. She looked happy.

"All right, we'll go to Second Avenue."

"Should I go upstairs to change?"

"No, you're pretty just like this."

Miriam snuggled more tightly to his side.

They went over the Williamsburg Bridge in the little trolley and then walked through busy Delancey Street to Second Avenue, all aglitter with red, green, and gold theater and restaurant signs. It was Saturday night, and people were already lined up at the ticket booths. Women in light furs were stepping out of limousines with their companions in front of the taverns and wine cellars. The air carried a mix of cigar smoke and perfume. The sidewalks buzzed with a happy, well-dressed Jewish crowd.

Here and there people greeted Nyezhiner, all people he knew. A writer with a wide-brimmed hat and a cane, an actor with a freshly powdered face and a white flower in his lapel, an actress with made-up eyes shining like lanterns—all smiled at him as they went by. So many happy faces, so many shimmering lights—that was Second Avenue in the evening!

Several steps led up to the Russian Bear. Inside, the large hall was ablaze with crystal chandeliers, ladies in fancy dress, white tablecloths. Miriam knew the café. She used to come here with David after the theater to drink coffee, look at the interesting people, and leave. Today she found herself sitting in a corner among the bohemians, writers and artists who didn't leave so quickly but instead sat talking for hours or looked toward the door to see if anyone interesting had turned up.

Moyshe Shteinman hurried over to their table. Moyshe Shteinman with a head as big as Beethoven's and a cane in his hand. Miriam had met him several times. Now he kissed her hand as though they were old acquaintances. In his mid-thirties, Shteinman was already considered a confirmed bachelor. He didn't work in a shop but lived in his father's house. He wrote only a few poems a year and had already read them aloud countless times both for his fellow writers and for actors. This kept him busy. He bragged that he was the only true bohemian of them all. Now and then he earned a small honorarium for a poem, and at such times he could be seen with a bouquet in hand, hurrying to the actress he adored. He would push his way backstage where the actress would allow him to kiss her hand and leave with a signed photo of her. In moments of bravado, Shteinman would take the photo from his breast pocket, still warm from his body, and proudly show it to his friends.

No one knew how Shteinman managed to attend all the premieres at the theaters and concert halls. He never had a penny to his name.

Now Shteinman sat down in the empty seat next to Miriam. She had to smile whenever she saw him. She knew he could be chivalrous to a woman without expecting anything more than to be allowed to kiss her hand. Even so, it was unpleasant to feel his hot breath, his bottled-up energy.

Shteinman sat for a while, breathing audibly. Soon he pulled a wrinkled paper from his vest pocket and handed it across the table to Nyezhiner. It was a short poem, eight lines, and Nyezhiner read it and raised his eyebrows with a slight smile, as if he'd heard a child speak wisdom like an old man. Yes, there was something unpolished and original in the poem. It was like a rare gem, raw and powerful.

"Well, Shteinman, you know I think highly of you. You keep it short and sweet."

Shteinman held his breath, savoring his happiness. He looked at Nyezhiner with silent wonder. He worshiped the man, would happily walk behind him and count his steps, remove a speck of lint from his shoulder, protect him and fight anyone who dared to say an unkind word about him, his poet, his prince. And he would stick up for not only the poet but also the woman the poet was attracted to. He wouldn't allow anyone to say an unkind word about her. He'd become her devoted defender.

Shteinman felt the softness of Miriam's gaze. Yes, he felt things deeply, and he knew that he and Miriam were one and the same in their feelings of wonder and admiration for Nyezhiner. He wanted to tell her that between the time he'd first seen her with Nyezhiner and now, he could swear she'd become even prettier. He would tell her now.

But his eyes were suddenly drawn to the opened door. Yankev Shor and a lady were entering the café. Shteinman had never seen this lady before. He forgot what he was about to tell Miriam. A wave of curiosity about the unknown woman silenced him.

The woman who'd come in with Yankev Shor was striking, with a slim, tall bearing and nice clothes. A gray woolen jacket lay over her narrow shoulders. At her throat hung a red fox collar that looked alive, its tail clenched in its teeth.

Shor said hello, his eyes crinkling in a smile as they always did when he greeted friends. Shteinman rose from his seat as he came over. But the waiter appeared and politely showed Shor to a newly empty table in the opposite direction. The café was now crowded with people who'd come in after the theater. Shor indicated that he'd stop by their table later.

Shteinman went back to his place, plainly curious. How could it be that he, who was always the first to know who was getting a divorce or who had a new lover, hadn't been aware of Shor's new woman? He wanted to ask Nyezhiner if he'd known, but Nyezhiner would never tell him; he'd just smile and wave him away. Shteinman kept stealing glances at the couple without saying a word.

Miriam, too, gaped at them curiously. But she didn't ask either. She knew Shor was spending time with Ada. A few days ago Ada had told her, laughing, that Shor had been to visit, bringing gefilte fish his wife had prepared. "He said his wife is an excellent cook, and he knew I like to eat and hate to cook." And Ada had laughed bitterly and added, "Very amusing, isn't it?"

Now Miriam fell silent. Somehow she felt personally offended. Yes, this woman was more elegant than Ada. But was that all that mattered?

The three people at the table were silently thinking the same thing but in different ways. A smile flickered on Nyezhiner's face. He remembered that Hershele Kalish had dubbed Shor "the Turk." And he remembered the evening at Hershele's apartment when Shor had seen Julia for the first time. Julia Polonski was a distant relative of Hershele's—certainly no reason for Shor to avoid flirting with her. As quiet and unassuming as he looked, all his friends knew he ran around with several women at once, even while happily married. His wife was no trouble; it was the others who gave him problems. His friends pitied him when he couldn't find his way out of a mess.

Nyezhiner told himself he was obviously the last one to preach morality. Everyone behaved the same way . . . as did he. Maybe he was even jealous because Shor was a "Turk," as Hershele said, and he himself couldn't keep up.

The waiter came over and Nyezhiner wanted to order something for Shteinman, but Shteinman assured him that he wanted nothing. He wasn't hungry.

Shteinman was on pins and needles. He wanted to go over to Shor. The dark face, the slim back, and the delicate bearing of the unknown woman sang to him a song of longing. Music and women—he'd hungered after both his whole life, pleading like a beggar and yet remaining alone. What did his friends know of loneliness? They had wives and also lovers. But no one had ever understood him and no one ever would. "Like a beggar . . ." There. He had the beginning of a poem.

Shteinman began humming to himself, seemingly lost in a trance. He was awakened by the clicking of a woman's heels and two golden cat-like eyes as a certain little actress, Bina, approached with quick steps. After her plodded a broad-shouldered man lazily chewing the stub of a cigar.

Shteinman rose and stood at attention like a soldier. He was ready to bow and kiss her hand, but she stretched out her hand to Nyezhiner instead, saying, "I knew I'd find you here! And I was right! I saw you as soon as I came in."

Nyezhiner introduced the two actors to Miriam. Shteinman offered his seat to the actress. She sat down without looking at him and barely glanced at Miriam. She didn't know with which of the two men Miriam had come, and she didn't care. She continued speaking to Nyezhiner.

"What a coincidence!" she said. "Today, after the play, Herman wanted to go to the bar, but I wanted to come here. I miss the days when we used to see you here all the time. Then you disappeared, gone without a trace. And now suddenly . . . here you are!"

Playfully, she ruffled his hair with her little hand, saying, "The same raven-black hair. The same eyes. Like daggers. You haven't changed a bit."

Nyezhiner smiled helplessly. At another time Bina's forwardness might have pleased him. Now, however, he felt Miriam's eyes on him and didn't know what to do.

Shteinman stood leaning on his cane. He glanced at Miriam's pale face but couldn't tell what she was thinking. Once again he was overcome by curiosity. Things had become very interesting.

"Bina," said broad-shouldered Herman, "the waiter is signaling. He has a table for us."

"Go ahead," replied the actress without turning her head. "I'll be there in a minute."

She had no intention of following him. In fact, she hoped that Shteinman would soon leave and take his little lady with him. She didn't like Shteinman. In the past, every time she'd sat with Nyezhiner, Shteinman had shown up and stuck to them like a leech.

"It's just my luck," the actress sighed. "I finally found you, but now you're about to slip away again."

She placed her small hand on his, hoping his eyes would look into hers, and sang out, "If only no one were here but you and me!"

Miriam made as if to smile, but no smile came. Her lips just parted slightly. How silly she felt. Would she have to get used to this? Would the women of his past—or not yet past—keep appearing out of nowhere? What was he feeling? Was he glad to have the actress fawning over him? Surely Bina must notice his embarrassment. But maybe he was embarrassed only because Miriam was there.

"This is ridiculous," Miriam said to herself. She wasn't used to such situations and didn't want to get used to them. She wouldn't stay here for another moment. He could stay if he wanted to.

She turned toward Shteinman. "Please give me my coat," she said.

"Miriam, what's wrong?" asked Nyezhiner. His embarrassed smile had disappeared.

Miriam didn't answer. Her insides were roiling and her throat had tightened. Never before had she experienced anything quite like this, yet the pain felt somehow familiar.

Chivalrously, Shteinman held her coat for her. But she took it out of his hands and ran to the door as if the floor were burning under her feet.

Nyezhiner followed. He looked confused, like someone trying in vain to solve a riddle.

At the door, he remembered he hadn't paid and turned back to look for the waiter. The tables full of people swirled around him. He saw everyone and no one. He didn't see the waiter who was standing nearby with a silver tray and a napkin.

Shteinman stared absent-mindedly as Nyezhiner left the café. He leaned more heavily on his cane.

Only then did the actress turn to Shteinman, as if seeing him for the first time. Maybe he could explain what had happened?

Shteinman spoke as if he were talking to someone else. "You—you've heard the news? Toscanini really is planning to play Tchaikovsky's Pathetique Symphony."

The actress shrugged.

« CHAPTER 7 »

1. THE MARQUEES were dark, the sidewalks almost empty. The wind carried pages of newspaper down the avenue. Here and there, a few people emerged from a tavern or a restaurant, their heels resounding in the nighttime quiet.

Nyezhiner stood on the steps of the café, his eyes searching restlessly for Miriam. Maybe she was waiting for him nearby? Silly. He knew she wasn't.

He began walking, taking long, quick steps. He'd overtake her, grab her hand and hold it tight. "Miriam, are you crazy? What did you do? Why?" He had no idea what had happened. He began to grow angry. He hadn't known Miriam was like that.

Here was the Williamsburg Bridge, and the trolley stops, with a few people waiting at each one. Miriam wasn't there. Maybe he should turn back to look for her? But where would he look? Maybe she'd gone a completely different way and he'd missed her. Strange how all this had happened out of nowhere, with no warning.

The tram came and he got on. He'd wait for her at Moyshe's house. That would be better. She couldn't avoid him there.

The five-story building on the corner was pitch black, its brick walls sound asleep. He looked up at the fourth floor. Was there a light? No, it was dark. They must have gone in different directions, and now he was here before her. He'd wait. No matter which way she'd gone, she had to come here.

He shoved his hands into his coat pockets and stood a while beside the building but soon grew impatient and started walking back to the plaza where she'd be getting off the tram. That way he'd see her sooner.

Trams arrived and passengers got off, but Miriam wasn't among them. What was going on? A strange thought ran through his mind: maybe she'd met someone she knew after leaving the café and gone someplace with him. Women sometimes took revenge that way.

He laughed at the crazy thought. In any case, he'd wait for her all night if need be.

He went back to the corner and stood under the streetlamp, feeling helpless. He asked himself what he should have done differently in that silly situation in the café. Should he have held himself aloof from Bina, to whose touch he had been anything but indifferent a year ago? Now the touch of her hand felt strange to him. But he did enjoy listening to her childish yet provocative words. Aha! That must be it! That was why he was hanging around here like a stray dog. That was what he was paying for. Well, all right.

He raised his coat collar and lit a cigarette. The screeching sounds of the trams in the plaza grew more infrequent. Seldom did anyone pass by. Suddenly it became clear to him that he was waiting for nothing. Miriam had managed to get home before he could catch up with her, and she must be asleep now. What should he do? He couldn't go to his room. He wouldn't be able to sleep anyway.

He stood glumly watching the building, without knowing why. A young couple came out of nowhere and stood at the entrance. They glanced at him several times as if they were waiting for him to go away. He straightened his shoulders and left.

His steps as he walked through the sleeping streets sounded hollow and empty, as if they belonged to a gambler leaving somewhere after losing everything.

He stood before the two-story house with furnished rooms. The building he lived in was fast asleep. The wind rattled the "to let" sign and engulfed him in a chilly gust of loneliness. He couldn't go up. He just couldn't. A few nights ago Miriam had been upstairs with him. Her hair had fallen onto his shoulders like a warm wave smelling of chestnuts. Her thin arms had encircled his neck. Her thin body had entered his skin, his blood. What had just happened? What demon was playing with him tonight? How could he make peace with this nonsense? He had to see her this very night! He had to make her understand.

He turned back toward Moyshe's. He would go upstairs. He didn't care if it was the middle of the night. He had to speak to her. She musn't think she could run away from him so easily and leave him alone. He could no longer be without her. She needed to know that. He'd tell her. Or would he? Such words embarrassed him. He knew women liked to hear such declarations, but he hated them. He knew he would end up saying the opposite of what he wanted to say. Still, he had to see her this very night.

2. The building was silent and shut tight. All the windows were dark. So was the hallway. He lit a match and looked for the buzzer. But all the buzzers were ripped out, as they were in most tenement houses. He didn't even know Moyshe's apartment number. Maybe it was on the mailbox. He knew it was on the fourth floor, in the front. Wait. One more match. There was the mailbox. He could see the name. But then the match went out. He lit another and suddenly felt a strong hand on his shoulder. He heard a harsh voice.

"Hey, mister!"

There stood a policeman with a flashlight, grasping his shoulder and asking what he was looking for in the middle of the night in this dark corridor. Had he lost something? Did he live here?

No, he didn't live here. Had he lost something? He wanted to explain what and who he was looking for, but suddenly he couldn't.

"You can tell us all about it at the station."

All at once Nyezhiner was seized with fear, a holdover from his boyhood in that other country, where he'd been beaten and imprisoned for reading Karl Marx and Bakunin. Why was he afraid now? This wasn't Russia.

Still, his hand trembled slightly as he pulled a newspaper out of his pocket.

Here was his picture. His name. He was not a thief.

The policeman used his flashlight to look at the picture and at him. Yes, they were the same.

"Why is your picture in the newspaper?" asked the policeman as if he had caught him red-handed.

He wrote for the paper, he explained. These short lines under his picture were his. A poem.

The policeman looked at the newspaper without a hint of understanding. Something about the strange-looking letters filled him with dread. They made him think of the old Bible, and of the old God. Yes, it did look like a poem. He had studied such things in school. And hated them.

He let go of Nyezhiner's shoulder.

Nyezhiner calmed down. Even smiled. He had the bizarre notion of reading his poem to the policeman. Was it possible the man was a Jew?

Once again the policeman asked what he was doing in this dark corridor so late at night. What was he looking for?

He was looking for the mailbox of his beloved, he said. He . . . she . . . he needed to leave her a note.

The policeman began to twirl his nightstick, and Nyezhiner understood that he had to leave the corridor. The policeman's job was protecting the nighttime peace and quiet.

Outside, Nyezhiner quickly came to his senses. What had he been thinking? To go into an apartment in the middle of the night and wake people up? Had he lost his mind? The policeman had been an angel sent from heaven to protect him from his foolishness. Thank God he hadn't gone upstairs. But he couldn't go home either. He would not sleep tonight.

He felt the policeman's eyes on him as he started off. He came to the all-night cafeteria in the plaza, opened the door, and went in.

Inside the cafeteria all was still. Silence hovered over the few customers sitting at metal tables like prisoners caught in a nighttime web. All that could be heard was a fly buzzing somewhere near the ceiling.

He ordered black coffee and sat down. A young man with a hardened face was sitting across from him at the next table, staring fixedly into the distance. Nyezhiner sat sipping his coffee with the same expression. The nighttime silence and the sound of the fly filled his ears.

How long did he sit? He didn't know. Outside the window, a gray morning began to dawn. The door began opening and closing. In came the fresh morning cold, the screeching of trams, and then the clanging of a firetruck. Nyezhiner stood up and left.

3. The firemen were gone, the clanging stilled. The reddish fog of dawn hung in the air. Through the fog he could make out the grid of the Brooklyn Bridge and, on the other side, the skyscrapers piercing the clouds.

The early morning cold made him shiver as he went back to the building on the corner. Hours ago he had decided to stand here, not to move until he saw Miriam. That plan was stuck in his head. He barely remembered what had happened between the two of them. The long, crazy night had mixed everything up, and none of it felt real anymore. All he knew was that he had to stand by the building on the corner until broad daylight, until he could see Miriam, and then all would be made clear. What exactly needed to be made clear he could no longer remember.

He stood next to the building with mouth clamped shut, face darkened, hat pulled low over his forehead, hands deep in his coat pockets.

Even though it was early Sunday morning, people had begun to bustle about the streets. Newspaper kiosks and grocery stores opened. Milk wagons clattered on the cobblestones. The firetruck went back to the station with silent bells. A woman opened a window and stuck her head out. No one paid any attention to him, a person standing next to the building. Let him stand. The day was moving on.

From a side street emerged a thin little chap with a camera on his shoulder. Right away he spotted his first customer, leaning against the building as if he were waiting to have his picture taken. He'd take the picture one-two-three and earn his first pay. His head was already under the curtain. With the speed of a magician, the man did his work. In a moment, he held a piece of wet tin in his hand. He didn't wait a second before approaching the wall. "*Mister, one nickel!*" He held out the tintype with its dark, stubborn image. The next moment, the print was in Nyezhiner's hand, and the photographer had left with his first payment of the day.

All at once the photo with the dark, stubborn figure aroused Nyezhiner's deadened thoughts. Maybe it was sheer coincidence that the photographer had shown up to take his picture, but now it seemed as if it had been planned. He would send the picture upstairs to her. It was for her. Let her see. Miriam!

Another seller appeared before him. A young boy with a pile of newspapers stretched out a hand. "*Paper, mister, paper!*"

Nyezhiner took a newspaper and extracted a coin from his pocket.

"See this, boy? Take a note from me upstairs and you'll get the whole thing. Fourth floor, in the front. You'll see this name on the door. Yes?"

The boy stood, tongue hanging out of his mouth, while Nyezhiner wrote on a wrinkled piece of yellow paper: "This is me. I've been standing outside your window for six hours. Mira, I'm not leaving. I'm waiting for you."

››››‹‹‹‹

How many hours ago had she hurried into the taxi outside the café? This is the end, she'd said to herself. I'm free now, and so is he. He and all his entanglements are no good for me. I'll run away somewhere, and he'll never find me. Why get involved in something so painful and uncertain? I'll get away and forget him. I have to. For him, I'm just one among many. Nothing more. Yes, this is the end.

But now that Miriam was looking at the photo, at his scribbled words, she was no longer the same as she had been hours ago. Neither was he the same. The photo showed someone with a pained face, a clenched mouth—someone who was hers, entirely hers. She couldn't run away from this face. All the beauty of his face seemed to have disappeared during the night, as if he had offered it up as a sacrifice to her, and now they were even. It came to Miriam in a flash that between them everything had a price. It was an eye for an eye, blood for blood, and until the score was even there would be no peace, no comfort. Things had never been even between her and David. He had suffered on account of her, but she had never suffered in return, had always kept her distance. It was the same with Nyezhiner and Chana. He owed her a debt he could never pay. Unless he suffered on her account the way she did on his, they could never build a life together.

Miriam ran down the stairs, her thoughts flying in every direction. My God, he'd stood all night in the cold! How could she have thought that this was the end, that she'd never see him again?

There he was at the entrance to the building, by the steps. It was him—and yet not him. His hat was crooked and low on his forehead, his eyes narrowed and yellowish. His lips had become thinner during the night, his chin covered with stubble.

She looked at the change in him. He looked both very different and very familiar. He looked ill. Was he feverish? She would put her lips on his forehead to check. But no, not here, not in front of the building. She stood for a moment, staring at him.

"Miriam, will you come with me?" he called out angrily, grabbing onto his lapels as if to rip them off.

Miriam had never seen him like this. But no, she felt that somehow she had indeed seen him like this—lost, with torn lapels. Dark as night. She felt herself following him into the dark recesses of his fevered mind.

Gently, she put her hands on his. His hands surrendered to her touch and fell helplessly away from his lapels.

She took his arm and they walked away from the building without a word.

In the garden in the plaza, Miriam put her lips to his forehead. His nostrils were trembling. Her face touched his, touched the stiff bristles of his unshaven beard, his dry lips smelling of tobacco.

Passersby turned around, staring at them. Miriam didn't care. They walked toward his room. Quiet hovered over them. The sun poured over the rising day. The earth smelled of spring buds, of calm. They could barely remember what had happened between them the night before.

« CHAPTER 8 »

1. THERE WAS NO denying that Yankev Shor had charm. The kind of charm that came from not achieving the success he wanted. A soft, sad smile hovered around his mouth as though he were forever apologizing, asking for forgiveness.

This smile served as a balm both for Ada's sorrow and for Julia's. His sickly wife, Mechla, depended on it, too.

Ada was tired. She dreamed of settling down with Yankev and his smile. With him, she thought she could find the peace that had eluded her earlier with more self-confident men. Yankev's humility made him the ideal person to satisfy her every whim. He might even be the ladder she could climb to fulfill her writerly ambitions now that her beauty had begun to fade.

Julia flew to every rendezvous with Shor as if on wings. Suffering from the indifference of her own husband with his insatiable wanderlust (at the moment he was with the Jewish Legion in Palestine, fighting for the ancient Holy Land), and disappointed by her previous affairs, she felt uplifted in her own eyes by her association with Shor, the poet and aesthete. His gentle lovemaking, the way he kissed her hands, entered into the very marrow of her bones. In the past, she had feared that her husband might learn of her affairs and leave her once and for all. Now she was ready to tell him the truth and leave him. She would write to Palestine to let him know. For the first time ever, she felt ready for such a bold move. All because of Shor.

Julia babbled all this to him, but Shor stopped her with his soft smile. Unfortunately, he couldn't accept her offer. She must know he had a sick wife and small children. He couldn't leave them. Even though at the moment he found her terribly interesting. In her eagerness, he said, she reminded him of Madame Bovary. What? She didn't know who that was? You know, the heroine of a novel. He would be sure to bring her the book. His wife, Mechla, was reading it now.

Julia laughed nervously. A bitter laugh—but how nice it was to be compared to the heroine of a novel. If things really couldn't be different, then they would have to stay as they were, and she would keep hiding it all from her husband. She could no more give up Yankev Shor, she said to herself, than end her life.

Julia and Ada, and his other liaisons and breakups with various women—all this gave Shor a sense of success he did not get from his writing. He often said as much to Mechla. Success and experiences of every kind, he said, deepened a writer's talent. Mechla would echo his words. "What can I do," she would say, "if my husband is a poet? Poets always need new sources of inspiration."

Mechla knew that any day now she might once again fall deathly ill, and then her Yankev would have to take care of her as before. That knowledge made her submissive and accommodating. She knew not to push him too far. She hoped that as he aged he'd settle down and stop chasing after new inspirations. She just had to be patient and wait it out. She would wait until he grew tired. Then he'd sit calmly at home and behave himself and be all hers.

Mechla never got her wish. Suddenly, Shor left his sickly wife and the children. The one at fault—as he confided to his friends, pulling down the corners of his mouth—the one at fault was Ada. She had so smothered him with threats about ending her life that he had no alternative.

Ada—how often the names of world-famous poets fell from her full lips: Pushkin, Heine, Verlaine, Baudelaire. She quoted them in the café. It never occurred to any of her writer friends that Ada herself was writing poems and sending them to journals. But all of a sudden a series of poems appeared in a political journal under a bold new woman's name.

In the café people speculated about who this could be. The name sounded like a pseudonym. Maybe a man was hiding behind that female name? The poems were not those of a beginner, let alone a woman.

The female name that sounded like a pseudonym appeared more and more frequently in the press. Finally it came out—it really was a pseudonym, and the person behind it was Ada. The same Ada everyone knew, though not by this particular name. Sometimes she'd use the names of the famous men with whom she was involved, and sometimes she'd use her childhood name. This name was a new one.

Now that the secret was revealed, Ada appeared in the café with a triumphant smile on her full lips. She sat in the very front, at the first table, her blonde braid atop her head, her small eyes reflecting the blue of the sky, and writers—even venerable ones—showered her with praise and addressed her by her bold new name.

Yankev Shor was among them, his soft smile hovering around his mouth. Deep inside he was embarrassed because Ada, with her handful of published poems, had made more of an impression than he had been able to with a whole book of poetry. Women! He wasn't, God forbid, jealous of her success. And in order to prove to himself that he didn't envy her, he began comparing her to the greatest poetesses of all time. Even to Sappho.

His humility made him feel all the stronger, like a worldly person, not a little man, and he liked that. Ada liked it too. She sensed in him the kind of support she had yearned for all these years.

Shor accompanied Ada home from the café and spent the night with her. He didn't go home to Mechla until dawn and completely forgot about his rendezvous with Julia.

In time Ada began to feel that he was hers. He shopped at the grocery store and even cooked various delicacies for her because she liked to eat and had never learned to cook. She bought him a pair of pajamas because she didn't like it when he lay in her bed in his underwear. But why did he need pajamas, Shor frowned, when he had to go home to Mechla in the middle of the night? He couldn't leave Mechla all alone.

At first Ada bit her tongue and said nothing. But how long could this go on? she asked herself. She wasn't getting any younger. The idea of sleeping alone all night made her shiver. The shivering came from a deep fear that one night he would leave her and never return. That had happened with others who had sworn to love her, but back then she'd been young. Famous men had wanted her. Nowadays she wasn't being pursued the way she had been. Of course she knew her shoulders were thicker, her back more stooped, her hips broader. She was past her prime, ten times more anxious than a young girl, afraid of being lonely. What would she do if she were left alone?

"Yankev," she said to him one night, feeling the chill on his side of the bed. "Yankev, you're leaving, and I'm afraid of being alone for the rest of the night. When I was younger, I wasn't afraid of anything. Now when I'm alone I'm lost. Lost, and no poem can comfort me. I wander around the house like a sleepwalker and talk to myself. I can't sleep. I bought myself a package of sleeping pills, and if you leave me alone tonight, I'm going to take them all."

Shor sat down on the bed again. Her wild talk had weakened him and filled him with despair. He shuddered. Yes, he said to himself, Ada was capable of doing such a thing to him.

"What are you saying, Ada? What kind of foolishness is this? 'I'm going away and leaving you!' How can you say such a thing?"

"But you really are going away and leaving me. I go crazy until I see you the next day. It can't go on like this. I'm not eighteen anymore. I don't want to be a mistress. I can't be. It's no secret to anyone, and certainly not to you, that I used to be married, that I've had lovers. You know their names. Famous men. The most famous. But they mean nothing to me now. They're garbage. Excrement. Mud. Do you understand?"

Ada buried her head in her pillow and from her throat came sounds of weeping, singing, laughing. Then she grew silent, as if she'd run out of breath. "Now you're all I have," she said, "and I want no one else. You are my last one, my only one. But you're living with two women. Maybe even with a third—with Julia. Oh, I know it! I feel it!"

Ada suddenly felt warm. She threw off the covers. Her pale skin shone in the dark. Ada always slept naked. She grabbed his hand, laid it on her hot face, her full breasts. His hand slid over her smooth, full body, and he fell on her without being able to stop himself.

››››‹‹‹‹

Shor stood in front of Mechla and spoke in a broken voice. He confessed that he was living with another woman. He defended himself: she was no ordinary woman. She was a writer. She had won him over with her eccentric ways, had bound him to her, and now he couldn't help himself. He was here now to tell Mechla his troubles and to take his things. It didn't mean he was deserting her. He would bring her his earnings every Friday. The other woman didn't need his money. He'd also stop by in the middle of the week on his way back from the office.

He wept real tears. Looking at his miserable face, Mechla felt moved. She cursed "the other woman" bitterly and brought him his clean underwear and shirts. Dependent and weak, Mechla realized that the most practical thing to do was to accept what was happening. He musn't become estranged from the house, from the children, from her. The door must remain open for his return.

Out of long habit, Mechla put some food before him. She

wanted to give him a few cookies to take with him in case he got hungry. But she refrained. She just told him he had to come home every Friday for fish and chicken soup. She and the children would be waiting for him. Once a week, they had to eat together at home.

And so he went home to Mechla every Friday evening for fish and chicken soup. He stopped by in the middle of the week, too. His children, Mendy and Eteleh, hardly noticed the difference. They hadn't seen much of their father before. On his way out, he would reassure himself that he was not heartless. He wasn't the only one in his circle who'd left his wife and children. Like them, he'd have an interesting life story.

When Mechla took to her bed with a weakened heart, Shor came every day to cook for her and the children. Her illness had made him learn to cook. He wanted to take some of the food to Ada, but he remembered that Ada must not know he had been with Mechla.

But Ada did know. She examined him closely, sniffed him and smelled Mechla. Something bitter penetrated her nose and eyes, and she cried that he was deceiving her.

Shor pitied himself. He regretted leaving Mechla and the children. Ada had chosen him only when she had no hope for anyone better. And yet she demanded his loyalty. She never cooked a spoonful of anything but was always snacking on sweets, growing fatter by the day. The house was a mess, her things in a jumble. Mechla's home was spotless. She washed his clothes and never demanded to know where he had been, or with whom. She didn't nag the way Ada did. He couldn't take it anymore.

"I'll go back to Mechla," he told Ada suddenly, his face twisted with grief.

Ada looked at him in shock.

"Go ahead. Tra-la-la-la," she sang out. "If you want me to end my life, I will."

She stood in the middle of the room staring into the distance. Her slip and stockings lay on the floor by her feet. Her housedress was open, and her naked skin was as pale as white, yeasty dough.

Shor was lost in thought. He saw Ada lying dead, her stiff, white body stripped of all desire. He shuddered. She could do it. She was capable of anything. How could he have such a thing on his conscience? Suddenly his lust awakened. Her wild words—that because of him she would end her life—whispered hotly in his ear, and as if in a dream, he knelt and embraced her round hips, crooning tenderly.

Ada's housedress slid off her round shoulders and mixed with the other clothing on the floor. With her eyes closed, as they rolled passionately, Ada heard him murmuring again and again: "My Sappho!"

2. Anka asked Julia to sit down. She smiled sweetly. She would just go to the kitchen to make some tea.

"No, no," Julia said quickly. "Nothing for me."

But Anka had already gone and returned with food. Julia was nervous. She had cleared her schedule in order to visit Anka when she knew Hershele wouldn't be home. She hoped to learn something about Shor from Anka. He had disappeared without a trace. She no longer heard from him or saw him. He had never called to explain why he hadn't shown up for their last rendezvous in Prospect Park. She'd waited by the gate in the lashing March wind for two hours until she began to cry. Later, in her room, she'd thrown herself on her bed in a fit, her fox collar around her neck, crying and laughing hysterically. She suddenly saw herself utterly bereft. It had been a long time since she'd received a letter from her husband. But she couldn't go looking for him, because he was far away, somewhere in Palestine. She wanted to find Shor. But where? She didn't even know where he lived. She tried in vain to find out if he had a telephone. She tried to excuse him: maybe his wife had fallen ill again and he couldn't leave home. Oh, she wanted to make excuses for him. Still, he could have left even an ailing wife for a moment and called her if he'd wanted to. Yet her telephone remained silent. She caught the flu and waited and waited. To no avail. Now it occurred to her that maybe Ada had something to do with it. Yes, she knew all about Ada. But that was over. He didn't love Ada. No one but she knew how he could love. Yes, she knew! It was impossible that he had forgotten her so quickly. He hadn't forgotten her. Something had happened to him.

Julia's eyes narrowed uneasily.

"Drink your tea, Julia. What are you so worried about?"

"Oh, I don't know. I haven't heard from Eliezer in weeks."

"Well, it happens. Letters are delayed sometimes, especially in such unsettled times. But don't think the worst."

"Who knows? He's been gone so long. Maybe he's found someone else." Julia laughed nervously. "It can happen." Maybe one of his friends had written to him about her and Shor, and now he wanted nothing more to do with her.

"Oh, Julia, you're not a child. You know full well that he needn't have gone all the way to Palestine to find a lover. He could have found one right here. It happens all the time. Everyone knows Yankev Shor has left his wife and gone to live with Ada."

"W-h-a-a-t?"

"Didn't you know? All the poets are talking about it. I hear she writes poetry."

Julia covered her mouth with her hand to keep from screaming. She felt that if she stayed there one more minute she'd become hysterical. She had to get out. She ran out of the apartment without saying goodbye.

Julia shook uncontrollably as she ran. She felt as if the street was about to crack open and crumble into an abyss. Her thoughts were in a jumble. Did she know Ada? Yes, she knew her from the anarchist circles of their early years. When she was just a young thing, Ada was already divorced. She went around with the elite of East Broadway and looked down on Julia. But by the time Julia grew up no one was looking at Ada anymore. Now it seemed she'd gotten her hooks into Shor somehow. But Shor loved her, not Ada. She knew it. Maybe Ada didn't know. Well, she'd soon find out.

Julia caught the tram from Brooklyn to Manhattan. She set off for Ada's in the grip of a feverish madness. The street, the house, the door. She remembered them all with strange clarity and yet as though in a dream. She'd often been to visit her old friends here, had often run into Ada coming or going with her fancy educated companions. Perhaps Ada was highly educated herself. Perhaps she could write poetry. But Shor loved her, not Ada. Ada had to know that. She would tell her face to face.

Calmly, ready for anything—she didn't know for what—Julia knocked on Ada's door. She heard Ada's sweet sing-song voice.

"Come in."

Ada was sitting at her work, with books and papers scattered about. She was barefoot, wearing a disheveled housedress. As usual when she worked, she was nibbling chocolate. She raised her little blue eyes from her work and saw Julia. She hadn't expected her. She opened her mouth, sticky from the sweet chocolate, and measured Julia up and down. She didn't ask her to sit.

Julia stood erect, ready.

"What do you want?" Ada asked coldly.

Julia began to speak feverishly. She didn't know what she was saying, but she knew it wasn't what she had been thinking of earlier. She heard herself say that she truly loved Shor. She had never loved any man so much. And she wanted nothing from him. Of course she didn't want him to leave his sick wife.

The cloying sweetness in Ada's mouth turned bitter. She stood up.

"Who are you to ask anything of him? It's impossible to carry on an intelligent conversation with you. How dare you come here to speak to me like this!" And Ada glared at her in a way that made Julia's whole body shudder, as if with just that one glance Ada had torn her well-fitting clothes off her body and spat at her.

Quickly, very quickly, words as sharp as needles shot out of

Julia's mouth: she would not give Shor up. No! No! That was what she had come to say. They would keep seeing each other because they were in love. That was what she had come to tell her! They would remain lovers as before. Let Ada eat her heart out. There was nothing she could do to stop them.

Ada began humming to herself, then broke off and ordered: "Get out!" And she went to open the door.

Julia stretched her thin body to its full height, shimmering and hissing like a snake, and spat in Ada's face.

At once, both women flew into a rage. They grabbed at each other's faces, hair, eyes—but couldn't reach them. Julia fell over a chair. Ada suddenly had a lamp in her hand and went for Julia in her bare feet. Julia managed to grab her hat off the floor and ran blindly from the apartment.

3. At home, Julia laughed, cried, laughed again, and cried again until she grew quiet and said to herself: "Ada's won. I've lost. Lost everything. Absolutely everything. What's the point of living?"

She rushed into the kitchen, locked the door, slammed down the window, and turned on the gas. She fell to the floor:

"To die!"

At first she felt strangely happy, as if she were cooling her heated heart. Let him remember her! Let her be on his conscience! Let their happiness be sullied. Good! Goodbye, world. Thirty years was a long enough life. Enough happiness. Enough lying. The world was disgusting. It stank. It stank of gas. It was good that she was still wearing her pink silk slip, her lace panties. When . . . they found her . . . she would be dead . . . Who would wear the dress she'd ordered from the seamstress? She'd asked her to make the neckline lower. The neckline would be lower, but she would no longer exist. Everyone else would still be there. He would be there. The park would be there. Ada . . . no, no, no, she didn't want to die! Not now! Another time, perhaps. Now she wanted to put on her new dress with the low neckline and go to the ball. She wanted to hear "you are as supple as a thin willow in the wind." She wanted to hear it one more time. She wanted to be as supple as a thin willow in the wind once more! She wanted air! She wanted to live, to scream. Why couldn't she make a sound? "The other woman" was eating chocolate. She would scream for help.

Sweat poured over Julia's body like a cold rain. The fear of death made her roll toward the door, toward the bit of air. But she no longer had a voice. She was silent.

››››‹‹‹‹

Gas blew into the hallway through the crack under the door. Neighbors knocked and doors opened, all except hers, which remained closed. The smell of gas was coming from there. People rushed into the hallway. Neighbors from other floors came running. And here was the super, the young Pole whom Julia greeted every morning and tipped generously. The noise had brought him running upstairs, but he'd forgotten his ring of keys. He rammed the door with his broad back and it tore off its hinges and fell toward the oven. On the floor lay Julia, her lips covered with white foam. The Pole stepped over her, turned off the gas, and opened the window.

A crowd filled the hallway. A policeman suddenly appeared and ordered everyone to disperse. The frightening clang of a firetruck could be heard, along with an ambulance siren. The building was besieged. The firemen administered first aid. The ambulance took her to the hospital.

The super put the door back on its hinges, checked to make sure it was closed, and went downstairs. Just then a telephone began to ring. The neighbors listened for a while, then locked their doors. It grew quiet.

››››‹‹‹‹

Julia was home from the hospital in less than a week. She was pale and gaunt, but her eyes glowed with a renewed desire for life and a fear of being alone. Now her older sister, a spinster with a big body and a gloomy face, came around more often. Julia clung to her, resting her head in her sister's hard lap, fantasizing about meeting Shor and feeling sorry that her sister's lap had never been softened by the sorrow of love. Out of shock and confusion, Julia began to think and speak with an intensity born of the shadow of death.

Two letters arrived from her husband. They'd been delayed. Happy, superficial letters. A shallow person, Julia thought. He didn't care about anyone. Still, the letters cheered her. She was glad he knew nothing, glad she hadn't lost everything, glad she wasn't alone. She picked up the low-cut dress from the seamstress, ordered a new suit for spring. She would be meeting with Yankev Shor soon.

Since the "accident," about which Shor had learned from Hershele, and since her return home from the hospital, he'd phoned her several times. Deeply moved by the tragic event, he began seeing her again, knowing that although their meetings had to remain a deep secret, Ada would nonetheless learn of it sooner or later. Somehow this didn't bother him. Let come what may, Shor said to himself, and turned to Julia with his soft, guilty smile. Because of him—only because of him—she had come close to death. Flaubert's Madame Bovary had poisoned herself and died. But Julia was the surviving Emma Bovary who wanted to suffer a bit more, enjoy a bit more. Maybe . . .

As he was thinking the thoughts of a writer, Julia was laughing and babbling incessantly by his side. But now he found her more interesting than before. She was a young girl who had learned to compromise and now wanted nothing more than what the day, the minute had to offer. He was touched.

He felt good around Julia now. She was easy, demanding nothing more than to see him, to be with him. Oddly, he began to confide in Julia about his bitter life with Ada. At once happy and unhappy, he and Julia stole away together whenever they could. Often they met as if by chance in a hotel outside town. Of course, Julia knew that these meetings had to take place in the greatest secrecy, but she had to confide in someone. She couldn't keep a secret for long—even when it concerned herself. Once, when she came to visit Anka, both to unburden herself and to see what she could find out, there on the table before her lay Shor's newly published book of poems, dedicated to Ada. Even though she'd known about the book and knew that Ada had gotten him to dedicate it to her by threatening suicide—still, when she saw the book with Shor's and Ada's names in gold letters, she felt deeply offended. She didn't go near the book. She just said to Anka, as if Anka knew all her secrets, "Will you look at this—he meets with me in secret, and then he openly dedicates the book to Ada."

She felt she shouldn't keep seeing him. She knew he was false. But she also knew that as soon as he called, she'd go running to him. He'd become a sickness from which she didn't want to be cured.

Anka was uncomfortable knowing Julia's secrets. Julia had to know she would confide in Hershele. And given that Julia's husband and Hershele were related, it would really be better for Hershele not to know. Anka said nothing and looked at Julia curiously. She was a puzzle, all right.

But somewhere deep in herself, Julia knew that although she was taking a risk by babbling to Anka so thoughtlessly, Anka would not betray her to her husband when he returned home, nor would Hershele. And even if they did, she didn't care.

Once Julia had begun talking, she went on. Shor had told her that Ada was sick and growing terribly fat, eating a lot of chocolate, crying all the time, no longer wanting to see anyone. Ada wanted to play out her drama for him alone; he was compelled to be her only witness. Anka smiled to herself. Shor was a strange man. He went through life responsible for three women, unable to break free, hiding his guilt behind a pitiful smile.

« CHAPTER 9 »

AT THE BEGINNING of June, New York was hot and steamy. Children played on the sidewalks and ran into the streets jammed with cars. There were no gardens or playgrounds in crowded Williamsburg, and Miriam counted the days until she could leave for the mountains with Dinaleh. All winter she'd looked forward to this time. David was glad to be free from worrying about the household and the woman who took care of his child. He gave Miriam enough money for her and Dinaleh to stay on a farm in the mountains all summer long.

As Miriam prepared for her trip, Nyezhiner felt left behind and deeply guilty about his own children, who had never been able to get out of town. He began spending more time in the neighborhood where his children played, buying them sweets, asking them about this and that. Then, suddenly remembering that Chana might be looking for them, he would take them back home and leave.

On one of those hot June days he found himself on their street, in front of the house where his children and Chana lived and to which he would never return. He'd come just to catch a glimpse of his family. He didn't see his older children on the street, but right near the steps he saw his youngest child playing alone.

He bent down to the child and patted him lovingly on his head, soaking up the sight of him, because usually he met with only the older children. Abeleh, barely three years old, looked up at him with a pair of large childish eyes and didn't recognize him. He seemed afraid of him.

"Abeleh, I'm your father." He picked him up. "Here, Abeleh, have some chocolate." But Abeleh didn't take any. He hung his head shyly and tried to squirm out of his father's arms. Nyezhiner held him tight. "Abeleh, look at me." Gently he lifted the child's face. Abeleh's lips quivered and he struggled to free himself. He began to cry.

Nyezhiner put him down, stuck the melting chocolate into the child's hand, and looked up uneasily at the window above. Maybe Chana had seen everything. He wanted to avoid her.

He left the street thinking things could have been different if Chana weren't so primitive, if she hadn't hounded him with her mad jealousy, if he were allowed to come to the house to see the children. But quiet little Chana went wild whenever she saw him, hurling whatever came to hand and hollering so the whole building could hear. It wasn't her fault, he would answer, that fate had so bitterly deceived her. She should have had a different husband, he would say, a different father for her children. After all, she knew nothing about him except the feel of his body. My God! Who had made such a mess of their lives?

He walked the length of the street arguing with his own conscience. Turning the corner, he bumped into Etka, the wife of his old friend Benya. He hadn't seen either of them in ages.

"What the hell!" Etka erupted. "I thought I'd bumped into a pole. You're so tall I have to crane my neck to see you." She laughed.

Etka had always been good at laughing. Even when she was poking fun at someone, her laughter was good-natured. Thin, short, with short hair and fingertips yellowed from smoking, she looked up at him curiously. In Yiddish mixed with Russian, the language she'd brought to America twelve years ago, she asked,

"What are you running away from? Are you coming from them?" And she looked him up and down.

"No," Nyezhiner answered abruptly in order to let her know nothing had changed. He took out his pack of cigarettes and handed it to her. Etka took a cigarette even though she never smoked on the street. He struck a match for her.

Etka looked at him closely as he stood bent over her. His gray suit was reflected in his green eyes, which seemed both sharp and distracted. His love affairs, she thought, had made him even more handsome than before.

Nyezhiner interrupted the silence. "You must be on your way to see them yourself."

"I am. But if it's really the measles, I'll be bringing it to my Yashinka."

"Who has the measles?" asked Nyezhiner.

"Abeleh, I think. I was there a few days ago. He had a rash and a slight fever. It looked to me like measles. I'm going over there to see if my diagnosis was correct."

"What do you mean, Etka? Abeleh is playing in the street. I was just holding him, and I didn't notice any rash."

"He's already playing outside?" said Etka, laughing again. "I guess I was mistaken, then. Or maybe not. After all, I did once take a course in medicine." And now Etka was laughing at herself. "I'll go have a look at your hero."

"Etka, I know how often you go visit them and how much you care about them, and I'm very grateful. I've always been grateful to you."

"Don't talk nonsense," said Etka, all but yelling to show how emancipated she was, how free of feminine sentimentality. In truth, Etka was very sentimental, curious about people—as women are—and deeply attached to her friends. She kept watch over all of them.

"So why haven't we seen you lately?" she asked. "Since when do we have to send you an invitation to come to us? Once upon a time, things were different! Do you remember those times at our house? Now things are so boring at home."

Of course he remembered Etka's home from years back. Her house was a nest of political exiles who were waiting for a sign that it was time to go back to Russia. Night after night they sat around smoking and talking. He'd spent many an hour with them. Now, in 1918, they were off leading the revolution, changing the world.

"Do I remember! Really, Etka, I feel guilty toward you and Benya. I'm always meaning to come to you, but, well . . ."

"People say they always see you with the same lady. So bring her along. We won't devour her."

"Well, Etka . . . I know. Thank you. Thank you for everything. Thank you whether you want my thanks or not."

He took her small hand and pressed it tightly. His eyes filled with tears. He bowed slightly and left. Etka looked after him as he walked away and thought things weren't so good with him, but they were worse for Chana.

Etka walked on slowly, lost in the memories that came flooding in one after the other.

There was the Sunday when Nyezhiner and Chana had come to visit them, the first time she'd seen them together. It was just after her marriage to Benya. What an odd couple they made. Chana: small, full-bosomed, heavy lips on a frozen face. Nyezhiner: tall and thin, with flashing green eyes, and a warm, approachable manner. She remembered how she'd looked at him, and Benya had said quietly, "Now you see why I didn't show him to you before."

She remembered answering: "You're right. It's a good thing you didn't."

Chana had stood there without moving a muscle, her round figure reminding Etka of a dressmaker's mannequin.

Benya and Nyezhiner had started talking politics and were soon immersed in their old, never-ending discussion. Benya liked to talk about subjects in broad terms, displaying his expertise in politics, literature, and all sorts of -isms, especially Marxism. Although he was a worker, Benya read more than he worked. He insisted that imaginative literature—poetry, novels—was only for simple minds. And so the two friends argued.

Benya spoke well, with a mix of fiery oratory and the style of a genial professor. Nyezhiner's talk went in all directions, full of the colorful images of a poet. The two competed to outdo each other in the artful construction of their sentences. They were careful not to speak in clichés or banalities. Very careful. Nyezhiner's eyes showed the pleasure he took in Benya's well-constructed sentences, his clear formulations and well-expressed thoughts. It was obvious that if Benya wanted to, he too could be a writer. But he left such matters to those with literary ambitions.

Both of them had tossed around quotations and raised their voices as if speaking to a large audience, even though only Etka and Chana were there to hear them.

Etka had looked at Chana while she listened to the conversation, which she'd heard before between Benya and his friends. She knew ahead of time how Benya would answer this or that assertion, how he would defeat his opponent. She even threw in a word or two on the opponent's side. Let Benya see that she had her own opinions.

Chana remained silent, and her face grew stonier by the minute. Nyezhiner forgot about her entirely. But when he suddenly caught himself and looked at Chana's frozen face, his desire for conversation was gone. Soon they said goodbye and went home.

Etka had stared at Benya as soon as the couple left. "What kind of couple is that? What are they doing together?"

"Who can understand such things?" Benya had answered. "It started before they came to America, when he was just a kid, a stutterer. I knew him when he first became class-conscious and joined the movement. True, even then he was writing those little poems. But everyone was writing poems back then, even me. Later we threw them away. Who expected him to become somebody?" All Chana knew, Benya said, was that she liked the seventeen-year-old boy next door. She was his age, maybe a year older or younger. Why he fell in love with Chana instead of any of the other girls was hard to say, except for the fact that being quiet and shy herself, she knew how to approach this shy boy. Maybe being neighbors had a part in it too. When her father found out, there was quite a fuss. He was against the match. What would a well-to-do Jew like him want with a boy from a poor family? Nyezhiner's mother sold chickens in the marketplace. His father hung around doing not much of anything. His whole family had an unsavory reputation.

The more her father objected, the more their love blossomed. Quiet Chana had a stubborn streak. After Nyezhiner spent six months in prison for revolutionary activities, her father, fearing the girl had already ruined her reputation, allowed them to get engaged. Benya remembered the gold watch and chain the young bridegroom received from his future father-in-law. Right after the engagement, he left town while she waited for him to send for her.

"And he did," Etka said.

"I don't know if he brought her over or she came on her own," Benya said. "Between the time he came over and the time she arrived, I didn't see him for several years. Maybe he missed the young girl he had left behind—or maybe he wanted to forget all about the match, but the gold watch and chain on his vest wouldn't let him forget. In any case, when I met them again, they were different, estranged from each other. A few years make a big difference at such a young age. Nyezhiner had changed more than she had. Spending two years in London and then coming to New York had cleaned him up and made him a new person. He'd made a name for himself and he—well, you saw him!"

"He's certainly good-looking," exclaimed Etka. "And so friendly!"

"And you saw *her* too. She's still young, yet such a cold fish."

"They aren't a couple, and she knows it. Women can sense such things."

"Well, in any case, here she is. They're husband and wife, and they will probably live out their lives together. Chana has the virtue of being quiet and submissive. How many virtues does a wife need?" Benya asked provocatively.

When she and Chana grew closer, Etka remembered, Chana had complained. "He doesn't love me. He barely talks to me, and I don't know what to say to him either." All he did, she said, was come home, eat, stick his nose in a book or sit with pen in hand, or his friends would come over and they'd go out and he'd come home late. She was lonely. She wanted to go back home to her father, but she was too ashamed.

Etka remembered the time when she and Benya came to visit Chana after her first child was born. They found her sitting calmly in bed as the baby nursed. As soon as Chana had weaned the first child, she had the next one at her breast. She never covered her breast when guests came, just like the women in the shtetl who would sit on the porch or the bench in front of their houses and nurse their babies for all the world to see. The great artists portrayed such women as madonnas. But times had changed, Etka said to herself.

Lost in her memories, Etka went on until she ran into Abeleh. He was still playing in the street, his hands and cheeks smeared with chocolate. Etka took his hand and led him upstairs.

She found Chana washing the floor with a pail of soapy water, brush in hand. Etka remembered that it was Friday and that she herself used to clean the floors for Shabbos. Chana's house smelled of Sabbath baking, Sabbath fish. Etka imagined that by cleaning the floors and preparing for Shabbos, Chana was expressing her hope that her husband, who had traded her in for another, would finally come back one of these Friday nights. Then all would be as it should be. Again he would come to her, again she would become pregnant, again she would give birth, again she would nurse a child.

« CHAPTER 10 »

1. THE SUN BURNED on the asphalt and the hot tar was steaming. The heat came from both above and below. Nonetheless, the city was at work, its people drenched in sweat.

As soon as the heat wave came, so too did an onslaught of work for Nyezhiner. Factories were bustling, machines were running, people were working until late at night and all day Saturday.

Nyezhiner usually worked only his regular hours, and sometimes not even that. On Saturday he stopped after half a day, took his jacket, and left. His quirks were well-known in the shops. Foremen were patient with him. Whenever there was a lot of work, quick, skilled workers like him were in demand.

This summer, however, Nyezhiner was working more. The workers and foreman winked at one another: "What do you know! He's bent over the machine just like everyone else."

Nyezhiner could see them winking, but he also knew that these days, work was good for him. Once Miriam left, he felt drained and empty, and work filled the emptiness. He had also lost the urge to go out in the evenings. After work he went to a cafeteria and from there to his tiny room to see if there was a letter from Miriam. There was a letter nearly every day—or, more accurately, a note. He would read the note so intently that it seemed like a letter.

Reading and answering the letters took up most of the evening, and after that he was too tired to go see his friends. After a day of hard work, all he wanted to do was sleep. He slept deeply, without dreams.

But on Saturdays he left work two hours early and hurried to see his children. They waited for him at a designated time near the entrance to the automat. (All except Abeleh, who was still too young to come.) His three daughters embraced him, greedy for a caress, a bit of fatherly affection, watching one another jealously. His oldest child, a boy, stood apart, embarrassed and pouting.

All the children loved the automat. What could be better? You put a coin in the slot, a little door opened, and you took out whatever you wanted. Their father gave them each a handful of coins, and they ran around happily for half an hour.

Then they all went to the big department store nearby so their father could buy them things they needed and things they didn't. The children knew the place well, having been there with him many times. The girls ran down the white marble stairs to the bargain basement to try on dresses, hats, coats, and more. They bounced excitedly from one place to another, wanting to buy it all. The boy followed silently, as if in a trance. They forgot all about him and didn't even notice when they lost him. When he turned up, Nyezhiner felt chagrined.

"Look at the soles of your shoes! Why didn't you tell me you needed new ones? Come!"

The boy walked along beside him, quiet and estranged.

In the big store, among hundreds of people, for an hour or two Nyezhiner was a father to his children. He laughed, joked, and had as much fun as the girls.

When they were done shopping, Nyezhiner realized he'd spent more money than he could afford. The rest of his earnings weren't enough to cover Chana's expenses and still leave a little extra for himself. He frowned. Well, he'd figure it out. He'd give the children whatever he had and find a way to borrow the rest. It was always this way. He waved his hand in the air and knew he would never change.

Once he'd put his children and their packages onto the tram and sent them home to Brooklyn, he felt very lonely on the crowded New York street on this stifling Saturday evening. Where should he go? To the café? Maybe Hershele and Yankev Shor would be there. He hadn't seen them for a long time. They were probably mad at him. First he'd been spending every evening with Miriam, and now he went home every day after work to see if there was a letter from her, after which he was tired and went to sleep. Tonight, too, he felt drawn to his room knowing a letter would be waiting.

He stood for a while on the corner debating with himself, then caught the tram to his neighborhood in Brooklyn.

2. Two letters were waiting for him when he got home. His landlady always brought his mail when she came to clean the room. Along with Miriam's letter there was one from Hershele. If Hershele was sending a letter, he thought, it must be urgent. A letter from him was rare.

He opened Miriam's letter first.

As usual, she wrote on lined paper, but this time her note was longer, more detailed:

"As you know, I've moved from the hotel to a farm on a mountain. From here, you can see even higher mountains and deep valleys filled with puffy clouds. It's beautiful, quiet, peaceful, and much cheaper than the hotel. Here I can be free of worries all summer. The farming couple have two little girls for Dinaleh to play with. They all go to sleep at sundown, and then I take a walk and think about you. I think about you more here than in the city. But the thought of you is somehow more painful here in the quiet of the evening. I'll try to stop thinking like this. I'll lock the door on those thoughts because I want to be good to you. After all, you have your own troubles. I'm not being unfaithful. Anyway, there's no one here with whom . . . don't be mad. I have to write what I feel and think. Otherwise . . ."

Having read the letter, he puzzled over the nuances, how she seemed to think there was some problem between them. He began to feel bad. He ran his fingers through his hair and sat a while on the edge of his bed. Then he stood up, paced the room, and suddenly took Miriam's letter and wrote his answer between her lines.

"The devil knows what I should do now. I'm so upset.

"Listen, if you feel the way you describe in your letter, then do me a favor and don't write at all, because with such feelings and such a letter you turn me into a pitiful creature, or a guilty one. I am neither. I don't want to keep a letter like the one you wrote. Read your letter again. How could I answer differently? I feel miserable."

Deeply agitated, he ran to the mailbox and sent back Miriam's letter with his words written between her lines. He felt empty and alone.

Coming back to his room, he felt every bone in his body aching. He lay down on his hard bed for a long time—he didn't know how long—staring out the window. Suddenly he thought of something Hershele had once said about Miriam—that she was toying with him. Then he remembered he hadn't opened Hershele's letter. It was lying at his feet, forgotten.

He stretched out his hand, picked up the letter, and opened it with a premonition that he was about to read something unpleasant. He was not wrong. Hershele's messy handwriting with its crooked letters attacked him right away:

"So! This is how it is, eh? The man blessed with a golden talent hangs on to the soiled hem of a woman's dress. He's forgotten his own worth! Forgotten his closest friend. Forgotten that he was supposed to come hear his friend read the eighth chapter of his work. Other colleagues came, but he, the one I have in mind with every word I write—he did not come. What is the value of literature when measured against his girl in the Catskills? Not much, eh? It's just plain wrong. How much longer will he keep this up? How did the famous poet put it? 'It's not the woman who grabs you by the . . . who is dangerous, but the one who grabs you by the soul.' She's the one to stay away from. She wants to conquer. And you, my dearest, most exalted friend, are a . . ."

Here were words that must not be printed, words that a man in the throes of anger yells aloud without hearing what he's saying.

Nyezhiner's fury mounted as he read. He grew rigid and almost calm. Calmly—or so he thought—he tore up Hershele's letter, and the clumsy, crooked scraps flew all over the floor. He lay back down on the bed, spent and exhausted, and closed his eyes.

3. He slept until the next afternoon, then opened his eyes to a gray sky that looked like rain. He noticed he was still fully clothed. He yawned, feeling dull and indifferent to everything, even to the intense heat in the room. But he couldn't lie there any longer. He got out of bed and saw the torn pieces of Hershele's letter. He stepped on them and suddenly shuddered. His dullness and indifference left him. He bent down to the floor and with trembling fingers collected the pieces of the torn letter. Unexpectedly, the spiky letters now seemed full of love. How had he not realized when he read the letter yesterday that underneath the hysteria of Hershele's letter was a friend who needed him because he had not yet found his own path, his own place in literature? He decided to go see Hershele at once.

Hershele needed him. And the truth was that he needed Hershele. As much as he neglected Hershele, he loved him just the way he was, the mad fool! He must be very unhappy to write such a mess of a letter. And so he forgave Hershele everything, all the nonsense he'd written in the letter.

Now, well rested, reflective, Nyezhiner was all goodness, all forgiveness. He wasn't even angry at Miriam anymore. He was sorry he'd sent back her letter with his ill-chosen words written between her lines. He would write her another letter right away. Maybe he should go to her? Yes, what a good idea! But he couldn't go until next Saturday because he had to keep his job in the shop. He had no choice.

"It doesn't matter whether you answer me or not. I'm coming! I'll leave here next Saturday at one in the afternoon, right after work. If you can, meet me at the train station. If not, I'll come find you, take a look at you—and we'll see what happens!"

He wrote the letter confidently. Addressing the letter to her in Mountainville, he could feel the fresh air of the open fields. He saw himself there, getting off the train, climbing a hill. Of course she loved him. He knew it. Strange to think that yesterday he hadn't been sure.

He shaved, washed with cold water, changed his clothes, and went down to the street.

Sunday. The Christian day of rest. The old Brooklyn houses were quiet, sunk in hushed devotion. A drunk wobbled by. The cloudy air was stifling.

He walked with his usual light steps, tall and thin, bowed down as if even his bones were lost in thought. He didn't lift his head, paid no attention to the street signs. He could find his way to Hershele's house blindfolded.

››››‹‹‹‹

As usual, Nyezhiner knocked on the door several times and entered without waiting for a response. There stood Hershele in his bathrobe, his eyes wide and shining.

Nyezhiner held out his hand with a smile, and Hershele took it nervously, his brow wrinkled with confusion. He was glad Nyezhiner was able to take the high road in response to his own hysterical letter. He looked surprised, agitated, and then he beamed, as if to say, "Now *here* is a great poet, behaving exactly the way he should!"

Rubbing his hands together, Hershele began practically dancing around the room. Anka came in from the kitchen, smiling broadly. "I knew you'd come!" she said. "I was just setting the schav out to cool and remembered how much you like that soup. I thought how good it would be if you came—and here you are!"

"Shor promised to come over today, in case you're interested," said Hershele, unable to refrain from the barb.

"Stop that," Nyezhiner said. "Come, I'll read you my new series of poems."

"What do I understand of poetry?"

"The same as I understand of prose," said Nyezhiner, eyes twinkling, and he knew they would exchange wisecracks without mentioning Hershele's letter.

They went into Hershele's study. Anka looked after them with a smile. She knew Hershele would read the latest chapter of his novel aloud. Nyezhiner might not say anything. He would lift one eyebrow and wave his hand in the air, and if he smiled, Hershele would feel on top of the world.

When Hershele was happy, it was like a celebration for Anka. But when he couldn't write and paced around his study in frustration, with the floorboards creaking under his feet, her mood would turn sour. She knew there was nothing she could do to help. She was glad whenever a friend came by and Hershele could read something to him. But she knew it wasn't the same as reading to Nyezhiner. When he read to Nyezhiner, he became truly uplifted, radiant. The truth was that her soul, too, was uplifted when Nyezhiner came by. Why should she deny it? She looked forward to his visits as much as Hershele did.

Anka busied herself in the kitchen, tasted the schav again, added seasoning, and waited patiently for them to emerge from the study, not daring to knock on the door and call them to eat.

When they finally came out, they both looked revived. Nyezhiner was gesturing. "Your chapter must go into the next issue," he was saying. "And since you like my third poem even though you don't understand poetry, it should go in the same issue. I'll dedicate it to you. When is Shor coming?"

"He promised to come this evening. But lately he promises and doesn't come," Hershele said. "Who needs dedications, anyway? What's come over you?"

And he rubbed his hands vigorously, his eyes sparkling in surprise, not knowing what to do with himself and all his awakened feelings. Suddenly he turned to Anka and said, "You're an honest soul. Tell the truth. Do you believe our friend when he says a poem of his is rubbish?"

Anka laughed. "Not one bit. And I've seen how his face falls when someone agrees with him."

Nyezhiner looked at Anka with a smile that said: Look how clever she can be when Hershele is in a good mood. She has me figured out.

At the table, the aroma of schav and green onions made Nyezhiner hungry. He was in high spirits. He'd done well to come here today. Every complicated thing now seemed simple. Any problem could be solved. Miriam's note and her mood, his return of her letter with his inserted lines—all seemed childish now. It was clear to him now that no matter how many times they lost each other, they would find each other again. He knew it. She might not know it yet. But she would.

He sat down at the table and said: "As you see me here, next Shabbos—for the first time since coming to America—I'm leaving this stinking city and going to the Catskills!"

Hershele inclined his beard like a question mark.

"I'm going to spend the weekend with Miriam. She's on top of a mountain. I don't even know what it feels like to breathe clean air. I'm so used to the dust and stink of New York and my stuffy room. The heat in my room is horrible!" He shook his head and smiled.

"I don't understand why you live in such an awful room," said Hershele.

"I don't understand it myself."

"I have a wonderful plan! It just occurred to me. Why not stay with us for the summer? My study is so airy and pleasant. You can sleep there. Anka, you could pamper him a bit with your cooking. Look at him—he's thin as a reed."

Anka smiled uncertainly. "He only likes my schav. All right, then, I'll cook it every day."

"I'm telling you, Anka, it's a great plan! He won't think so, though."

"Hershele, are you serious?" Nyezhiner asked. "You'll give me your study?"

"What else could I mean? In the summer I only work for a few hours a day. That's when you're in the shop anyway. In the evening the room is yours!"

"I accept! Your desk calls to me! I just hope you don't come to regret this."

"Anka, bring us the bottle of schnapps. Let's get him drunk!"

Hershele felt wonderful now, with no room in his heart for anger. Even his bitterness toward Miriam was gone. He felt pity for them both.

4. Nyezhiner had been sleeping on the sofa in Hershele's study for three nights. Every day, straight from work, he ran to his awful little furnished room to see if there was a letter from Miriam. But no letters arrived from her and he left with head bowed. In fact, he could have figured out there wouldn't be any letters this week because of the letter he'd sent back. Maybe she was insulted. Maybe she was waiting for his arrival in order to have it out with him. In any case, the cheerfulness he'd felt a few days before had deserted him. He went to his room at Hershele's, but reluctantly. Once again he felt detached from everything. Now he didn't want to show his face to Hershele, or especially to Anka. She prepared food for him, and he left it untouched. He couldn't eat and hadn't

slept for several nights. He felt weak and wished he were alone, away from the two of them.

A separate door led from the hallway to the study. Hershele had given him the key. Tonight, depressed, Nyezhiner crept through that door into his room like a thief. Thank God, they didn't seem to hear him come in—or maybe they did but understood that he wanted to be alone.

The door to the dining room was closed as usual, but he could hear laughter, talk, the clatter of teaspoons and glasses.

He sat down at Hershele's desk. He had to write another letter to Miriam. He picked up a piece of paper and wrote:

"Since receiving your letter, to which I responded with insults—because I found nothing but insults in your letter—I've been beside myself. I can barely sit still at work. I'm not eating and I haven't been able to sleep for several nights. What did you have to do that for? Now I'm calmer, so I don't believe you really meant what you wrote. What, then? Are you trying to provoke me? Why? You don't need to take revenge. My blood is your blood. All this carrying on—do you think I've wronged you? Are you trying to get something out of me? Let's stop! Unless . . . I don't know . . . maybe I still don't really know who you are. If so, that's my fault, and I'm ready for anything. I'm writing and crying. Yesterday I was at a complete loss, and so I didn't dare write to you. I hope to receive a letter from you that will calm me down. Or I can leave my work at any moment and come to you, talk to you, even die."

He finished writing, held his head in his hands, and was ashamed of his own tears. He would be embarrassed if Anka or Hershele were to open the door. They were both devoted to him, yet he felt pathetic, like some hapless boarder.

After a while he became as calm and quiet as when he was about to write a poem. He sat, attentive to his own pre-writing quiet before stretching out his hand to take up his pen.

On the other side of the door he could hear Julia's voice, her high-pitched laughter. There were guests. People were speaking loudly. They mentioned the names of friends, but not his name. The telephone rang—perhaps for him? No, thank God. If Anka were to knock on the door and invite him to drink tea with them, he'd beg off. Thank you. Thanks. He couldn't now. He wasn't feeling well.

« CHAPTER 11 »

1. BETWEEN THE FARM and the mailbox, a narrow, well-worn path ran through the meadow. Miriam walked there every day, seeing no one. Now and then a frog jumped across the path or a bird fluttered into the air with a frightened cry. The sun caressed her neck and arms. Miriam liked the aroma of the fields and enjoyed her walk because it had a purpose: to put a letter into the box and get her mail. The mail consisted mainly of a letter from Nyezhiner, or sometimes two. When there was no letter from him, Miriam knew nothing important would happen that day. She'd carry out her routine with Dinaleh, all the while thinking about him.

It had been two days since she'd received a letter from him. And because in his last letter he had returned hers, he might never write again.

All at once the mountains, the trees, the grass—they too had nothing to say to her. Now she knew she wouldn't be able to stay there for long. She'd thought all she needed was to be with Dinaleh. Having her child with her, taking care of her, would keep her here forever. How little a person knows about herself... Just a few days ago she'd thought that now, far from him, she was free of him, of his power over her, his will. And that since they were already apart, maybe it wouldn't be too painful to stay apart. Strange: they were so close, and yet she still couldn't convince herself they were meant to be together forever. His wife and children hovered over her like clouds. So did the woman for whom he had left his wife. It seemed to her that their closeness was only temporary, that it would have to end.

Such were the notions that flooded over her, out here with the blue sky and the stillness of the forest. Only a hint of these thoughts had gone into her letter to him. What had she expected? That he would seize the moment and end it: "You're playing games with me? Then it's over." Or that he would offer a new sign of his love, thereby freeing her of the doubts that had grown sharper here, in the quiet fullness of trees and fields? What had she expected? She didn't know, but now once again she was walking through the field to the mailbox with a quivering heart. Was there a letter from him? What if there wasn't?

She came to the dusty country road. The mailman stopped there every day with his horse and cart. Here, in the tin box nailed to the trunk of a tree, there should be a letter for her.

She glanced into the box. No letter. Nor any of the newspapers she received from the city. Once again she must have come too early. She would wait.

She stood in the shade of a tree. The dry, dusty road climbed into the distance. Fields in every shade of green stretched out before her, dotted with farmhouses slumbering in a quiet as old as the world.

Beside her the road lay as still as though it were listening for a squeaking wheel, a trotting horse—or perhaps it was she herself who was listening.

All of a sudden the dusty road began to vibrate. The squeak of wheels and the rhythmic clop-clop of hooves could be heard. A cloud of dust arose, and the mailman with his horse and cart stopped before her.

"Good afternoon, Miss!" The mailman's dry voice rang out in the dry air. He didn't get down off the cart.

Miriam went over to take the bundle of newspapers and letters he was holding out to her. He knew her, knew that the papers and letters were all for her. The farmers rarely received letters. The summertime guests did. He knew everyone who was spending the summer in the surrounding farmhouses. He seemed only to be passing through, but he knew everyone's secrets. He knew who was coming, who was going, who was respectable, and who was a sinner here among the farmers and the city folk alike. He knew everything, kept quiet about everything, and if he spoke, it was about the weather.

"We need some rain."

Miriam noticed dust from the road in the creases of his face.

He pulled on the reins, the wheels turned, and Miriam stood with the mail in her hands. Two letters with Nyezhiner's fine, neat handwriting stood out from the pile.

Which should she open first? He never dated his letters. She had to figure out from the contents which letter had been sent first. "I don't believe you really meant what you wrote," she read. "What, then? Are you trying to provoke me? Why? You don't need to take revenge. My blood is your blood."

Miriam read the two letters almost as if they were one.

"I'm coming on Saturday to speak to you . . . even to die . . ."

Miriam smiled. Such nonsense! And yet—how lovely, how powerful, how piercing his words were! Her blood ran faster in her veins and washed away every doubt she had about him, about herself. She had to have him near her always—if not himself in the flesh, then at least his words with their hot, tearful vigor. Otherwise she would waver and stray, give in to her doubts and have nothing to hold on to, nothing to believe in. These words of his enveloped her and gave her courage, strength. She would need that strength if she were to continue to walk this difficult, uncertain path with him.

Miriam reread both letters. She breathed in his tears, his despair, and she became calm. She went back to the farm, and the mountains greeted her and seemed more majestic, prouder, as if the white clouds were encircling them with tender caresses. Whom should she tell that he was coming? Not Dinaleh. The child was waiting impatiently for her Papa, who had written to say he was coming to see her soon. He would take her to a nice hotel near the *layk* and drive her around in his new *kar.*

Dinaleh came running. She saw the letters in Miriam's hand and joyfully called out: "A letter from Papa?"

"No, my child, not from Papa. You got a postcard from him the day before yesterday."

"When is he coming?"

"We'll find out when he writes."

"When will he write?"

"I don't know. Maybe tomorrow."

Dinaleh frowned and looked with idle curiosity at the letters in her mother's hand. Instinctively, Miriam tightened her grip on the letters. She'd go upstairs to her room and read them again. Why had the two letters arrived at the same time? Well, it wasn't the first time a letter had been delayed. At times her letters to him were also delayed.

She had to think of a place for him to stay. He certainly couldn't stay with her on the farm. She had only one room. He knew nothing about hotels in the mountains. She had to start thinking about that. She had to find a room for him.

2. Every Friday the farmer harnessed his horse to the cart and went into town to buy food and other necessities. This time his wife reminded him to buy fireworks. The next day was the Fourth of July. Last year all he had done was shoot blanks from his gun and that was that. But this year she wanted fireworks. She held his eye longer than usual and that meant: we have a guest this year, so we can afford it. Let's treat ourselves.

The two little girls, Mary and Anne, stood by silently, their blue eyes looking up at their father.

Miriam rode into town with the farmer. She had things to buy, but she also planned to stop by Sophie's Hotel in the valley to ask about a room for Nyezhiner. She could see the hotel from her window up in the hills. By day it was a white spot in the green valley. In the evening, when the hotel's windows were lit up, the building looked like a ship floating in the fog. Now, for the first time, she'd go into the floating ship.

Sophie, the hotel owner, met Miriam in the lobby and peered at her with pale little eyes in a freckled face. Her bare throat and hefty arms were sprinkled with freckles too, and her coppery hair was done up in a perm. She shook her head. No, she had no rooms available. Everything was booked over the July 4 weekend. But it was possible that someone might cancel a reservation and a room would open up. Let him, the one for whom the *yung laydee* wanted to reserve a room, come by. He wouldn't find a room anywhere else. "We'll see," she said. "Don't worry, *hun-ee*." And she threw Miriam a knowing glance.

The farmer waited impatiently. He tugged on the reins, flicked his whip. He had to make up for lost time. It was already late. Miriam could hear him muttering to himself.

His wife, Mabel, had worked in the hotels as a girl, he was saying. She was a "*chaymbermayd*." The hotels were full of nastiness and sin. They multiplied like toadstools.

Miriam said nothing. She'd thought that as a last resort she might ask the farmer if he could offer a room to a guest coming from New York for a day or two. Now she knew she couldn't ask. She was hiding a transgression and didn't know if she'd be able to hide it indefinitely. So she kept quiet.

In town, among things she needed, Miriam bought something she didn't need: a bottle of perfume. Why would she need such a thing here in the country, amid so much aromatic natural growth? She didn't ask herself the question and didn't need to answer it. But somewhere, in the fog of her uneasiness, she knew that she wanted to make herself more attractive to him.

On Saturday it was very hot. The sun rose like a ball of fire. The trees and grasses were still. Miriam bathed in the woods, naked. She could be certain no human footsteps would come near the waterfall under the spreading branches of an old tree. No cows grazed there and no one could be seen for miles around.

Afterward she dried herself in the sun, feeling her long hair waving in the hot wind and caressing her shoulders and back. Today she would wear her cotton print dress. She wanted to look good for him.

When it came time to go meet him, Miriam was worried about everything: not knowing exactly where he'd be staying; keeping Dinaleh in the dark; keeping the secret from everyone on the farm. The farmer's wife had promised to watch Dinaleh and feed her lunch while Miriam was at the train station "meeting a friend from New York." Now, all dressed up, Miriam stood before the woman and saw a look on her face that said: "No one gets this dressed up for just anyone. One woman can't fool another."

Miriam turned away and shrugged off her uneasiness. She took the shortcut down to the station. The farmer couldn't take her with his horse and cart and there were no buses, so she would walk the two miles.

The sun stood high in the sky. The path was dry and dusty. As she set out, her freshly powdered face was pale with uneasiness and expectation. The farther she walked—the only person walking this dusty path—the more the hot sunshine settled onto her face and body.

An hour later, when Miriam arrived at the train station, her dress was sticking to her body and sweat was running down her sun-drenched face. She wiped at the sweat with a handkerchief. She was the only one at the station. No one else was in sight. Everything looked empty and forlorn. A breeze wafted over the rails stretching into the distance, and Miriam turned her hot face to the cool air. Her dress blew upward and no longer clung to her. Her body cooled, but her face was still red hot. Her eyes widened with anticipation.

She paced back and forth on the empty platform, paying no attention as the plaza filled up with automobiles, horses, and carriages. Summer guests had come to fetch their loved ones. The place was full of wives and children, waiting impatiently.

The minutes passed slowly as they waited, eyes straining in the direction the train would come from. People checked their watches, muttering that it was late.

Suddenly there came a dreadful whistle, and from far away came the train, snaking its way toward them with its black smoke billowing over the treetops. The hissing, gasping locomotive brought with it a warm, human joy.

The crowd surged toward the train. Drivers hurried forward to claim their guests for the hotels. Women and children pushed to greet their husbands and fathers. In the midst of the tumult Miriam spotted him getting off the train, his eyes searching for her.

In that moment, all her uncertainty and uneasiness disappeared. Here he was, standing before her face to face. They kissed lightly on the lips, clasped hands, and stood staring at each other, their gaze separating them from everything around them.

The platform was noisy and bustling as people picked up their boxes and suitcases. The train was already gone, trailing a streak of black smoke.

One last time, drivers called for the guests coming to their hotels: *Swan Lake, Rabinovitch's Hotel, Sophie's Hotel.*

Miriam took his arm. "Come!"

Four people were already sitting in the automobile going to Sophie's Hotel, including a fat couple with double chins and the oily red hands of fishmongers. The woman had nowhere to put her large arms. In front with the driver sat a young man with a hot, eager face. He looked impatiently out the window, stretching his neck in his stiff collar and new tie. He couldn't wait to settle into the hotel and start enjoying the pleasures that awaited. In another corner sat a thin woman, not young, who looked lonely. Her pointy chin and tightly pressed lips seemed to say: "You never know what can happen on a summer vacation—even to a girl like me."

Miriam decided that if there was no room for Nyezhiner at Sophie's Hotel, she'd ask the driver to take them somewhere else.

The two of them felt out of place in the car. What were they doing here?

« CHAPTER 12 »

1. SOPHIE LIFTED HER pale eyes to look at him. Here in the lobby by the cashier, he looked as if he had fallen from the sky. With a pleasant smile and a bit of a stammer, he asked if she had a room available for a day or two.

His long, pale face, his half smile, his attractive whiff of foreignness won her over immediately. Who was this stranger? Why didn't she simply tell him all the rooms were taken? He stood there waiting: tall, thin, bent like Christ on the cross. Why was it that she instantly felt him awaken something inside her—feelings that were both motherly and girlish? Clearly she couldn't send him away. She called the bellhop. "Take the gentleman up to room 12. Ten dollars in advance for two days, please."

As she wrote down his name, Sophie once again regarded him with the eyes of both a mother and a young girl.

The bellhop looked for a suitcase to take upstairs, but Nyezhiner hadn't brought one. He held on to his leather briefcase, which contained several notebooks of poems and a new pair of pajamas.

He followed the bellhop, signaling to Miriam that he would soon return. Sophie looked after him curiously and threw Miriam a sly glance. Miriam forced herself to smile and waited amid the unfamiliar bustle of the lobby.

On the veranda, a waiter began to ring what looked like a cowbell but sounded harsher, more grating. Some guests returned from their walks; others got out of their hammocks and came in from under the trees and the banks of the brook. From every direction, guests came streaming in for dinner.

Heavyset, hairy men just out of the water lumbered through the lobby. Big women with blubbery stomachs came through with their chubby little children. To Miriam, they all looked both familiar and unfamiliar. She had lived among such people in her childhood, and she recognized their type: fishmongers, herring sellers, hearty butchers—hardworking people with healthy appetites.

Someone turned on the gramophone and a lively tune began to play. From sunburnt bodies, hairy chests, and blubbery stomachs emanated a lust for earthly pleasure.

The doors of the dining room were wide open, and the aromas of chopped liver, chicken soup, strudel, and condiments wafted outdoors.

Nyezhiner came downstairs after washing up. Here, among the crowd, he seemed ethereal, otherworldly. He looked on as the healthy Jews with ruddy necks and barrel chests streamed into the dining room. A warm feeling for their physical strength and fullness engulfed him. But something cried within him, a wish for at least one of them to recognize him, to know who he was. He, who had been raised from their depths to sing about them, to tell stories, to cry.

A short fellow with broad shoulders raised his sunburnt face and looked him in the eye as if to ask: "Who is this guy? What's he doing here?"

Miriam stayed for the meal, for which Nyezhiner paid in advance. A table was set for the two of them, as all the others were full. The room was buzzing like a beehive. Waiters scurried by with heavily laden trays as the diners looked on hungrily. The room fell silent when the eating began, but after the first few dishes had been consumed, the crowd began humming a happy tune that mingled with the tune on the gramophone in the lobby.

It wasn't only the humming or the clatter of dishes, the music or the clapping of hands that kept Nyezhiner and Miriam from talking. It was simply that there was no need to talk. Why speak when they could look into each other's eyes, their fingertips touching? Nyezhiner ate little. (He could seldom eat without embarrassment.) Every few minutes, the waiter came by with a loaded tray, but Nyezhiner touched Miriam's fingers more often than the food on his plate.

After the meal, Miriam led him along the path toward the farm. They crossed a narrow footbridge and entered the woods. Here Miriam brought her lips to his. For a while, they stood like that, intertwined as if they were one person with two beating hearts. To avoid getting carried away on the path where someone could see them, Miriam led him farther into the woods, through the pine trees and thorn bushes to a green mossy expanse that opened up suddenly near the waterfall. It was the small piney woods she'd described in her letters. Here she often came with Dinaleh to splash in the water that ran over the smooth rocks.

He followed her, bending his head under the branches. A bird screeched and fluttered from branch to branch. "Look," Miriam said, "from here you can see the most distant mountains and the sunset."

He stood intoxicated by the mountains that he was seeing for the first time. The quiet—such quiet! The smell of the pines and the wildflowers. The feel of Miriam's hand on his thigh . . .

He felt entirely calm. He looked around. Under his feet, the grass lay as soft as a carpet. In the dappled light, the lush surroundings reminded him of a freshly tidied house. As if he had just come home, he took off his jacket, shoes, tie. Miriam slipped off her shoes and they walked barefoot over the cool, soft grass. Smiling, he pulled Miriam down to the soft grass as if onto a well-made bed.

››››‹‹‹‹

Miriam opened her eyes and saw that the sun had gone down behind the mountains. Streaks of gold, purple, and red filled the sky, the colors changing moment by moment. Soon they would merge and night would fall. Nyezhiner was asleep on her shoulder, as calm and trusting as a child. She remembered that she had left Dinaleh alone for many hours. Guilt made her get up. Moving softly, she gently removed his head from her shoulder, picked up the hairpins that had fallen on the grass, and began putting up her hair. Her shoes were soon on her feet, her dress straightened. When he opened his eyes to look at her, he wouldn't see anything amiss. The heat, the nakedness they had just known, was now like a dream from which they were waking. It was good. This was how birds behaved. Birds spread their wings, shook out their feathers, and sat on their separate branches, lost in their birdlike thoughts.

Miriam stood lost in thought with a hairpin between her lips. Nyezhiner was no longer asleep. He looked at her calmly. Their eyes met. No, it had not all vanished in a dream. What had been before was still alive in his eyes, and perhaps in hers as well.

"You're so good to me, *dushka,*" he said, calling her his darling. "More than I have a right to expect. And what will you do with me now? I'm entirely in your hands."

"I'll send you back to the hotel until tomorrow. I have to go back to Dinaleh."

"But I want to see you again today. Tonight, I mean, after Dinaleh falls asleep. I'll wait for you here."

"It will soon be pitch black here, and you won't be able to find your way back to the hotel."

"I don't need to find the way back. I'll stay here."

Miriam smiled.

"If only I could take you to my room for the night . . . but I can't. You understand. And don't wait for me, because Dinaleh will be staying up late for the fireworks. She's waiting. I have to hurry."

"Well, yes, of course. It's the Fourth of July. I forgot."

He was already dressed, and Miriam fell into his arms. For a while they embraced, ready to forget themselves once more.

A bird suddenly fluttered its wings. A drop fell from a swaying branch. Miriam tugged on his sleeve.

"Come. It's getting dark."

They walked back to the path, his hand on her shoulder, her hand touching his leg. Miriam felt she could hear his thoughts.

"At night," she said, "if you can't sleep, look up and you'll see the light in my window. I can see the hotel from my room. Here is where I have to turn toward the farm. If you follow the path into the valley, you'll come to the hotel. You can't get lost."

"Maybe in the morning you and Dinaleh will come to the hotel and we'll have breakfast together?"

Miriam thought for a moment.

"No, I have a feeling that wouldn't work."

"All right, do what you need to. I'll find my way here early tomorrow morning. I'll sniff out the spot."

They kissed again and went their separate ways.

2. In the evening Miriam sat on the veranda of the farmhouse looking down into the valley, which was engulfed in fog. The outlines of the mountains were barely visible, and Sophie's Hotel with its blazing windows reminded her—as it did every evening—of a ship floating on the nighttime sea.

Suddenly the stillness of the dark-blue evening seemed to quiver. Loud bangs could be heard coming from the mountains, and across the way other mountains echoed with their own small bursts of thunder. Golden dust lit up the darkness for a moment; small flashes of lightning fell somewhere in the distance.

It was the farmers celebrating the Fourth of July. But those familiar with the area knew that the farmers wouldn't make much of a fuss over the holiday. They left that to the city folk, the hotel guests. They were the ones who would celebrate, but not yet. The guests were still busy eating. By the time they made their way to the dance hall, the farmers would already be asleep. Then the party would go on until late at night.

Dinaleh was restless. She kept running back and forth between the veranda and the kitchen. The farmer's family was only beginning their dinner of pork with cold leftover potatoes, and they were in no hurry. Why rush? When their little display of fireworks was finished, the holiday would be over for them.

But Dinaleh was impatient. She kept asking when the festivities would begin. Finally the farmer's wife took off her apron. Mary's and Anne's hair had been combed earlier into tight braids. The farmer got the fireworks and they came out, all of them cool and calm. Only Dinaleh was ready to explode with anticipation.

The farmer's family lined up on the veranda like soldiers. Dinaleh looked at the farmer's hands and saw him take out a small, tightly wound ball with a wick like a snake and throw it up into the dark sky. The ball unrolled, quivered, sparked, and went out.

Dinaleh was disappointed.

But now the farmer was throwing all the balls up, one after the other. Five at once! Five fiery snakes unraveled, quivered, sparked, and became red-green dust that dispersed like seeds in the nighttime sky.

The farmer clapped his hands. He had fulfilled his obligation: celebrated the Fourth of July. What more did he need to do? His horse was in the stable and the field was dark.

"Good night," said the farmer, and then his whole family said good night. It was time for bed.

Miriam and Dinaleh stayed out on the veranda. Dinaleh looked disappointed and her face seemed to ask: "Is that all?"

Miriam gave her a hug. "Wait a bit and you'll see fireworks!"

Dinaleh didn't answer.

At that moment, a rocket burst over Sophie's Hotel and spread like a peacock's tail over the night sky. Soon the peacock's tail dissolved into golden stardust. The sky was shot through with colorful powder, and a golden rain fell.

"Look, Dinaleh!" said Miriam, happy for her child.

Dinaleh showed no particular joy, as if the whole celebration up in the sky was something foreign, not hers.

Why was Dinaleh so quiet? Could it be that her disappointment with the farmer's fireworks had caused this mood? Miriam gently encircled Dinaleh's shoulder.

Later, upstairs in their room, when Dinaleh was asleep, Miriam brought the lamp closer to the window. She stood and looked down into the valley.

What was he doing now? Was he looking up to the mountain, seeking the light in her window?

3. Right after breakfast, the farmer harnessed a horse to a carriage, and his wife came out dressed in her Sunday best, a hat on her head. Mary and Anne had blue ribbons in their braids. They all got into the carriage, and the farmer tugged on the reins.

Were they going to church or visiting friends? Miriam didn't ask. Dinaleh was jealous. She stood, mouth ajar, eyes wide. When the carriage had driven away, she burst into tears.

"I want to go somewhere!"

"When your papa comes to see you, he'll take you places in his car. You like that, don't you?"

"But I want to go right now!"

"Right now we'll go to the woods to pick berries. And we'll have a guest there. Do you know who? He brought you a present last winter, a paint box. Do you remember Nyezhiner?"

Dinaleh didn't answer. She pouted.

When they came to the waterfall in the woods, Miriam had a feeling that Nyezhiner was there or had just been there. The mossy spot under the tree had recently been flattened. Or was it still like that from yesterday?

Dinaleh was splashing among the stones near the waterfall. She was used to playing alone, and even to inventing her own toys. But now and then she became cranky and lonely, like any only child.

Miriam went out to the open path to look for Nyezhiner. Maybe he was wandering around lost? Suddenly she saw him creeping through the undergrowth. He was collecting wild strawberries and popping them into his mouth.

Miriam laughed and he looked up, surprised. He hadn't heard her coming. He straightened up and smiled.

"I'm absolutely drunk from the air here and the surroundings."

He put a wild strawberry into Miriam's mouth, and after looking around carefully, they kissed.

"Did you get lost?"

"No, I followed my nose and came straight to the woods. I've been creeping around here for I don't know how long."

"Did you sleep well?"

"Maybe ten hours. I collapsed into bed early and woke up with the sun."

"So you didn't hear the fireworks?"

"No, nothing. But I saw such a sunrise today! Miriam, if only I could stay a little longer. But early tomorrow I have to be back at work in the shop."

He drew her to him and Miriam looked around.

"Dinaleh is here in the woods with me. I couldn't leave her. There's no one at the farm now."

"Oh, if only I'd known."

Suddenly Dinaleh was standing before them. She ducked her head shyly. Miriam gave her a hug.

"Say hello to our guest!"

Dinaleh didn't speak.

Nyezhiner took her by the chin.

"Let's take a look at you. Beautiful! Red cheeks! And you've grown. I think you're already as tall as my Soreleh."

"Where is Soreleh?" asked Dinaleh curiously.

"At home in Brooklyn."

"Why is she in Brooklyn?" Dinaleh pressed.

Miriam glanced at him. He seemed a bit lost trying to find an answer. Miriam answered for him.

"Why not bring Soreleh here? It just occurred to me this minute. She can stay as long as she wants. Simple! I don't know why I didn't think of it before."

"Would you really want that?"

"Why not? Soreleh isn't a little baby."

"She's older than Dinaleh."

"It's a wonderful idea. Dinaleh enjoys older children. She likes to follow them around."

"I don't know. It might work. Perhaps?"

He thought about it. It wouldn't be easy to get Soreleh away from Chana for a few weeks. Still, it was worth a try. The air here would brighten Soreleh's pale face. She was the palest of all his children, the most delicate.

Dinaleh and Nyezhiner quickly became friends. As was his wont, he treated the child like an equal. Dinaleh was soon holding his pencil and notebook and drawing figures. Every now and then she ran to show him her pictures, and he exclaimed over her skill.

Miriam and Nyezhiner sat under the tree where they had lain yesterday. They touched so Dinaleh couldn't see them, looking into each other's eyes.

"What did you do all morning?"

"I was here," said Nyezhiner, smiling. "I recognized the hill, the tree. I lay here and read. The grass was still damp; the hill was familiar. It was mine."

Miriam pressed his hand. When he was near her like this all her doubts and uncertainties disappeared. As soon as she was alone, her unease and uncertainty returned.

"I wanted to surprise you and come to the farm very early," he said. "I held off. I didn't want to bother you. But I'm very curious to see where you live."

"Let's go there now. I'll show you the farm and my room. It's everything a village should be."

"With you I'm not embarrassed to be a greenhorn. I've never seen a farm in this country."

On the way to the farm, all three of them picked berries. Miriam led him through the field, between the haystacks and the rows of corn. She showed him the garden with the beans and cucumbers, the chicken coop and ducks. He walked by her side like an outsider, a stranger, a city dweller, an absentee landowner inspecting his property.

A frog sprang suddenly out of the grass near him and he startled. Dinaleh laughed gaily. Such a big person afraid of a little frog!

Later, Miriam took him up to see her room. Her cozy room with its pair of plain, wooden beds, its two high windows looking down into the valley. For a while they sat on the edge of the bed. The feel of his hand in hers made her close her eyes. It was so easy for her to forget herself with him, give in to the moment. But the thought that Dinaleh might find them made her stand up. Avoiding each other's eyes, they went down to the yard.

It was time for lunch. Miriam carried some food to the oak table under the apple tree. She brought sour cream for the berries, bread, cheese, and a pail of cold water from the well. She did everything with quick movements, as if she were dancing. He looked at her, and something sang within him. Meanwhile he chattered away with Dinaleh, playing word games with a nervous joy. All of a sudden he said to Miriam, "I'd be embarrassed to write poetry here." And he gestured at their surroundings as if he could say no more. Before the great beauty of God's world, he could only be still.

Miriam always felt more fully awake around him. Not only his words and his voice but his very thoughts were as clear to her as the clearest waters.

The three of them sat at the table under the apple tree. The mountains were shrouded in mist. The sun stood high with a veil of clouds over its hot face.

The three at the table were lively, happy, but each of them was holding a secret sadness.

All at once the farmer's family arrived. Mary and Anne jumped down from the carriage. The farmer's wife got down slowly, looking askance at the three of them. Miriam began to stammer. She pointed to Nyezhiner: "Yes, that's him, my friend from New York."

Nyezhiner was already standing up and bowing to the family. The two little girls gaped at him. The farmer unhitched the horse and led it to the stable without looking at anyone.

Suddenly Nyezhiner felt uncomfortable. He quickly said goodbye as if he didn't belong there. Once again he felt that he didn't belong anywhere. Even the little spot in the woods that he had come to love now seemed foreign. There was no doubt that it belonged to this farmer who wouldn't look at him. He and Miriam had merely stolen it for a while. Well, how else could it be?

Suddenly his longing for words returned to him like a longing for home.

4. Dinaleh fell asleep early because she'd been up so late the night before. It wasn't yet evening, but the chickens with their beady eyes had already settled cozily into their roosts. Miriam knew the farmer's family would also go to sleep soon. Still, she asked the farmer's wife to listen for Dinaleh because she had to take her friend, who was going back to New York, to the station.

Without looking up, the farmer's wife reminded Miriam that, as she knew, they went to bed early.

Of course she knew. She'd probably be back before then.

Miriam thought the farmer's wife was smiling to herself. Doubtless she didn't believe her. But at that moment it didn't much matter. She hurried to meet Nyezhiner at their spot in the woods before it became dark. They would steal time to be close once again. It would be good to feel the warmth of his body again, to snuggle with him like birds in a nest.

Miriam came back to the farm much later than she had intended. The farmhouse was dark, and she crept in on tiptoe so no one would hear her. She wasn't worried about Dinaleh. The child almost never woke up during the night unless she was, God forbid, sick.

Miriam opened the door to her room. The full moon shone through the window. Dinaleh wasn't asleep. She was sitting up in bed, her face hidden behind her hands as if she were praying. Suddenly Miriam remembered that when Dinaleh went to sleep early, she often woke up in the night. She had completely forgotten.

"Child, what's the matter? Why are you up?"

Dinaleh burst into tears. She didn't know why she'd woken up. She'd called for Mama, and Mama hadn't answered. Then she saw that the other bed was empty and she was frightened by the empty bed and the whiteness in the window. She thought Mama would never return, and she was asking God to send her Mama back.

"Silly girl! I was here, right by the house, saying goodbye to Nyezhiner." He was going back to New York at dawn, and he'd asked her to kiss Dinaleh and say goodbye for him.

She kissed her daughter. "Ma, sleep with me," Dinaleh sobbed.

"Of course, whatever you want."

Miriam changed her clothes and got under Dinaleh's covers. Dinaleh gave one more little sob and fell asleep right away in her mother's arms.

Miriam lay awake. She asked herself where the child had learned that there was a God and that one could pray for something. And another thing: Dinaleh had never asked Miriam to sleep with her. That must have come from her jealousy of Nyezhiner. She had to be more careful around the child. When the three of them lived together, she would sleep in a room with Dinaleh, not with him. She would steal away to his room, always steal away. But now she wasn't worrying about that. She was calm but sleepless.

Night turned to dawn. All was quiet. The crickets stopped chirping. Only a glimmer of moonlight remained. A rooster crowed.

From a distance, a train whistle and the chugging of a locomotive broke the quiet. The wheels ran rhythmically on their tracks, and the rhythm rocked her to sleep. In her sleep she knew it was the train. The train that was carrying him away.

« CHAPTER 13 »

1. A HEAVY SUMMER stillness hung over the gardens and fields. The birds in their nests were silent. An apple could be heard falling from a tree.

Miriam read the letter very slowly. It was the first letter from him since he'd left at dawn that other morning, and inside her she could still hear the whistle of the train, the hissing of the locomotive, the rhythmic movement of wheels on rails stretching far away. It all came back to her as she read.

"Imagine, I could have stayed with you all week! A branch of our workers is on strike, so I'm not in the shop. But what can you do? There was no way to know. I feel good, though. And I feel you so strongly that I embarrass myself! I do feel good. So sadly good because I feel you so strongly. And good because I feel that you feel the same way. Oh, how strange! I'm not just talking myself into it, am I, my little Beetle? It's blood! It's you and me! And I'm so thankful for the two sacred days we spent together that I feel like bowing to the ground. The little annoyances there, what we didn't say, how little we were able to see each other, the way we sometimes misunderstood each other—these are all things that had to be. And the slight bitterness is dissolved by all that we experienced together in that other world, far from the noise of the city. Isn't that so, Beetle? (That's my nickname for you.) Answer me and tell me if I'm fooling myself. Oh, I should have stayed. We have so much to talk about, to understand about each other.

"I got to the station too early, so I ran back up the path to you. I ran to the footbridge. I bent down and splashed water on my face, looked up at the mountain and called—almost yelled—Beetle! Then I ran back to the train. Arrived. Still had to wait. Paced back and forth, but still I felt good. But we had to see each other one more time, so it was good that you came running down the hill. Go to that hill often—it's our hill. Where shall I kiss you? Wherever I kiss you will be good."

Miriam's mood matched the fullness and calm of her surroundings only as long as it took her to read his letter. After that her uncertainty and fear returned. Her life stretched out before her, and the future looked utterly mysterious and unknown. Why hadn't she had such thoughts when she was with him? Maybe she should go back to the city. But how could she take Dinaleh back now, during the heat wave, to wander the fiery streets of New York? It wasn't her daughter's fault that she felt so restless here and had too much time to listen to her own thoughts. If they went back, she would never be able to make it up to Dinaleh.

Miriam's feelings poured into the letters she wrote Nyezhiner, letters brimming with a girlish longing that only he could still. Uneasiness and longing filled her days on the farm. Today she waited on the path for the postman, who arrived and departed in a cloud of dust. Now she had two letters in her hand, and from the two envelopes with their different handwriting two different faces looked up at her: one Nyezhiner's and the other David's.

David's letters were always addressed to his daughter. Dinaleh always opened them herself, but she couldn't yet read, so Miriam read them to her. If David had something to tell her too, he always addressed her in the third person, sounding angry. If Miriam didn't want Dinaleh to hear those lines, she would skip them.

If Dinaleh were with her now, she would have read David's

letter first. But Dinaleh was in the garden with the farmer's wife and daughters, filling baskets with vegetables to carry home. Miriam took deep breaths while she read Nyezhiner's letter, in which he wrote:

"From morning until I go to sleep, I think of you, I see you, I speak to you openly, sincerely. My little Beetle, don't be sad. I'm looking at you! Here I am sitting and looking at you with comforting eyes and I'm holding you tenderly. Good? So be happy! I have so much to write in my poems, but I can't. I'm too busy with thoughts of you. Is that so bad? What use are poems anyway? No, no, my girl, without poems I'm useless. And you're useless too if I don't write. It's you and ... poems. So now I guess I'll sit down and write. It's been a long time since I did. I've even forgotten how. But I'll do it!

"I want to send you a sweater, but it will take too long to get to you. So what will you do if it gets cold? Let me know, and I'll send it right away.

"Be well. Be calm. I kiss you here, and here, and here."

Now she did feel calm. Calm because of his loving words. She wished she could close her eyes and lie in the hammock until morning, until another letter came from him. And do the same every day until summer's end when she would once again be in the city, in a new home with her child, with Nyezhiner always at her side, and with no time to think because she would be busy only with him. Always only with him.

Now here came Dinaleh, running toward her and grabbing her father's letter from her hand. Opening it and giving it back to be read aloud. He wrote that he missed her—so he was taking a week's vacation and coming to see her. He'd take her to a big lake where they would stay in a nice hotel for a week and drive around in his new car.

Below that, he wrote in the third person that she should get the child ready, and he'd come for her next Friday. He hoped there would be no objections. He did, after all, have the right to have his daughter with him for a week. If she didn't trust him to take care of Dinaleh, she could come with them if she liked. It was a new hotel, and they could get an extra room for her and Dinaleh if she wanted.

Simple words. But the calm that Nyezhiner's letter had produced in her was totally erased by David's letter. Tomorrow was Thursday, she realized. Between today and tomorrow she had to decide whether to send Dinaleh away with David and remain alone or go along with the two of them. What should she do? If only she could ask Nyezhiner for advice. But if she were to write him today, her letter wouldn't be posted until tomorrow. Too late. And, anyway, what advice could he give? He, the prince of words, was helpless when it came to everyday matters. He might not even understand what all the fuss was about. Hadn't she already left Dinaleh with David for six months? True, but in those days she went to see her every day. And there was a woman taking care of her. How would a man know what to do with a child, even for a week? And what would the farmer and his wife think if she were to stay here alone? They didn't know anything, and she had no desire to tell them her life story. No, Nyezhiner would be no help in this situation. Strange that she hadn't anticipated any of this. Clearly she had no alternative but to go with them. And she had to let Nyezhiner know right away.

She sat down to write Nyezhiner another letter. Two in one day. She described the problem and concluded with her decision to go with Dinaleh. Like a governess. What else could she do? She couldn't even wait for his answer because it wouldn't arrive until Monday. He shouldn't worry about her. She would write him from there and send her new address.

2. Chickens scurried around the farmyard on little yellow legs, pecking at kernels and worms. From time to time a couple of them would get into a fight, and the air would fill with fluttering wings,

flying feathers, and loud clucking, while the ducks waddled away to the pump.

Dinaleh was looking out the window at them. She'd had a stomachache and diarrhea all night. Miriam was in the kitchen cooking something for her. She'd told her to lie down. But Dinaleh was too impatient to lie down. If she couldn't go to the garden with the farmer's wife and daughters to pick the bright red tomatoes and the knobby cucumbers she loved to chomp on, then at least she would stand at the window and look at the ducks and chickens. And maybe Papa would come soon? Suddenly, the ducks hurried away from the pump, flapping their wings, and the chickens flew off. A car drove into the yard. David got out and looked around. This had to be the farm, but there was no one in sight.

Dinaleh knocked on the windowpane, calling out, "Papa!"

Miriam came into the yard and wiped her hands on her apron. She knew David was coming today, but she hadn't expected him so early. She'd decided that Dinaleh couldn't go because she was sick. Dinaleh's illness had solved the problem, she thought. Now the child couldn't go anywhere. David stood before her like an uninvited guest. His broad shoulders, his square face, his brown eyes looked both familiar and unfamiliar. The two of them tried to smile and couldn't decide whether to shake hands.

Finally David asked, "Where is she?"

At that moment Dinaleh ran down in her nightgown and jumped into his arms. He bent down to catch her and she buried her head in his shoulder. They hugged each other tightly and kissed.

Miriam stayed at a distance. She thought it was a good thing the farmer's family wasn't there to see her standing apart from her child's father.

"What's the matter with her?" David asked.

"She has an upset stomach."

"For long?"

"Just since last night."

"Does she have a temperature?"

"No," Miriam assured him.

"I'd give her a little castor oil," David advised without being asked.

Dinaleh frowned. "But it doesn't hurt anymore!"

David looked at Miriam for an answer.

"I don't know," said Miriam, as if to herself. "I don't think we should take her anywhere in her condition."

"Maybe I should take her to a doctor, just to be safe?"

"I don't even know where to find a doctor here. Let's wait for the farmer's wife to come back. I can ask her."

Dinaleh burst into tears.

"Why are you crying, child?" David asked. "I came to give you a *gud taym*."

"But I don't want to go to the doctor!"

David thought for a moment. "Here's the situation," he began, as if he were talking to no one in particular rather than to someone standing right before his eyes. There was no phone at the farm, and it wouldn't be convenient to leave and come back. Miriam must agree that the child didn't actually seem ill. So the best thing would be to take Dinaleh with him, but he'd feel more secure if Miriam came along. In the hotel it would be more comfortable for the three of them to be together. It was a big place, and no one looked into another's business. And though with any luck they wouldn't need it, there was almost always a doctor among the guests. If not, he had the car and they could figure out what to do. What did she think? Was he right or not?

"Yes," she said, "maybe that would be best under the circumstances."

"So what are we waiting for? Let's go. Will it take long for you to get ready?"

"No, the suitcase is already packed." She just wanted to give Dinaleh something to eat, a little rice to stop her diarrhea.

"It doesn't hurt anymore, Ma!"

Miriam didn't entirely believe Dinaleh, but she didn't want to torment her with more questions. And anyway, if the child wasn't well, it made her feel more secure to have David nearby with his car.

As she was getting dressed, she felt somewhat uncertain about what she was doing. But she brushed her doubts away. Going along with David and Dinaleh seemed like the easiest thing to do. The decision had been made. She shouldn't overthink it. She shouldn't expect herself to be an Übermensch.

David leaned against the car, waiting for them like a chauffeur whose job was to transport them from one place to another. When Miriam came down, he hurried to take her suitcase. It was the same suitcase he had always carried for her, and for a moment he felt he was playing the role of her husband. Or maybe he was just fooling himself? He blushed. It suddenly became clear to him that during all his years with Miriam he had always been playing a role.

They avoided each other's eyes. But Dinaleh was cheerful. She was the first to jump into the car.

Suddenly the farmer's wife and daughters arrived with their baskets of vegetables. Dinaleh yelled happily, "Here's my daddy!"

Mary's and Anne's eyes grew round at the sight of the shiny black car, and they kept staring at the impressive machine. The farmer's wife was curious too. Miriam had told her she might be going to the big hotel by the lake for a week. Now Miriam called out from the car, "Mrs. Brown, meet Mr. Eidelberg." She had no need to add "my husband." Dinaleh had already said "my daddy," saving her the trouble.

Mrs. Brown stared more intently at David. Miriam could see she was comparing him with the guest from New York.

The woman's staring eyes made David uncomfortable. He put his foot on the gas pedal and the car began to hum. Miriam just managed to tell Mrs. Brown that Dinaleh was feeling better.

The car's rear wheels began to spin, and in a cloud of dust they set off along the open road.

3. Miriam looked silently out the window as they left the mountains and the farm and descended into the valley. The car seemed to swallow twenty miles in no time, and suddenly there appeared before her eyes a large, oval lake. David skillfully turned the wheel and pulled up in front of a sprawling white building.

Their roles had switched. David got out of the car as if he owned the place, and Miriam stayed huddled in the car feeling like nothing more than a governess to her child.

The hotel manager met David with a smile. David apologized: he had reserved just one room for himself and his daughter, unsure whether his wife would be able to come. But now here she was, and they needed two rooms. He wiped the sweat from his brow.

The hotel manager kept his thoughts to himself. The hotel was new, but he was an experienced manager, and he betrayed not a shred of curiosity about his guests. He only regretted that at the moment he happened to have no adjoining rooms. The only rooms available were across the hall from each other.

"That's fine," said David. He liked the lake and wouldn't look for another place. And he wiped his brow again.

They went up to their rooms and closed the doors. David might never have crossed the threshold of Miriam's room, but Dinaleh developed a fever, and David came in with a doctor and then with medicine from the pharmacy. He sat with Dinaleh while Miriam went down for meals.

By the third day, Dinaleh was up and playing by the lake with her father. Alone in her room, Miriam wrote a letter to Nyezhiner. She had written him on the day she arrived. Now she told him that Dinaleh felt better and had already made a friend. It looked as if the child would have a good time for the rest of the week. She herself would endure it. The week would pass and soon be forgotten. Had he received her two letters? Had he written to her here at the new address? She was waiting impatiently.

Her letter was short, matter of fact, a little dry. She didn't want to linger over her embarrassment, her regret over coming here. What was done was done. There was nothing more to do.

On the fourth day, Miriam went to town with David and Dinaleh to buy a few things for the child. David generously paid for everything. He looked pitifully happy. Were they back together again? Had she encouraged him by coming here or by how she was behaving? That very morning she had let herself be coaxed by Dinaleh into a rowboat and had spent time with them both on the calm lake. David's loneliness had moved her. She was afraid that if they were alone for a moment, he would break down and she wouldn't be able to help taking pity on him. So she'd proposed going to town to buy things for Dinaleh. Constant movement was important, with Dinaleh between them. The two of them must not be alone.

At lunch, when they came back from the lake, the manager handed Miriam two letters. David stood beside her. His neck and shoulders stiffened. Just then the lunch bell began to ring, and Miriam put the unopened letters in her bag. David followed her into the dining hall and sat down stiffly at the table. Dinaleh was the only one who ate heartily, like someone after an illness. Miriam gave her some of her own food.

David told the waiter the coffee was cold. Then his face went gray, as though he were in pain, and he left the table. He sat on the veranda hidden behind a newspaper.

Dinaleh went to play on the swings with the other children, and Miriam went up to her room, closed the door, and threw herself on the bed. She opened her bag and took out the two letters, compared the dates on the envelopes, and opened the first. The letter had been written on a wrinkled piece of scrap paper, and Nyezhiner's handwriting looked somehow different.

"Since receiving your letter with your new address and the weird name of the lake, I've been beside myself. I wrote you an angry, unfortunate letter like the one I wrote a while ago, but then I took myself in hand, tore it up, and calmed down a bit. I'm still not calm, though. I keep repeating to myself: 'Be a man.' Beetle, I'm not working today, so I slept all day, because everything is awful. What you're going through makes me very worried. Yesterday I had no letter from you. If only I knew what was happening with you! I'm writing you as always, but each time I have to write your new address, I feel . . . well, you understand. Even though I know I'm being foolish, I'm going to mail this letter and then go back to sleep. It's hopeless for me to try to do anything. If I don't get a letter from you tomorrow, I'll be miserable. I have a headache.

"Well, take care."

Miriam's heart beat fast and her left ear turned red, as if she had been slapped. She grabbed the second letter in hopes that it would calm her. But it had the same altered handwriting, and that worried her. Her eyes raced over the lines:

"Don't worry about me. I'm just '*crenky,*' irritable, and in such a state that I look like a lost soul at a stranger's wedding, like a worm in horseradish. That's exactly how I feel. Irritated and at my wits' end. If you were in town, in my present state I'd undoubtedly be standing under your window all night. As it was, I went to bed at nine o'clock, listless and unable to sleep.

"What's wrong? I don't know. But I'm right, though I don't know who I am or what to do. I do know how silly it is to write to you when I'm angry and upset. But I must, or I can't write to you at all. I can't lie to you. I've felt like this the whole time you've been at your new address. And now? Well, I'm not doing well. I'm in the right, and you're ignoring that, so I'm making a fuss. I know things aren't good for you either, but I'm too hurt right now to deal with your feelings. You are how you are. Well, so be it. Oh, your letter! So clever, every word just right—with the upside-down stamp! How terrible I feel! So what is there to do? Should I stop writing to you? Tear up what I've written? Run out of Hershele's apartment? It's raining, Beetle. I'm sick. I have a fever . . ."

Miriam's eyes filled with tears. Her lips quivered. My God! She hadn't expected this. She hadn't predicted he would react like this. How different he was from everyone else she knew! How he tortured himself and those closest to him in the name of honesty. And in truth he was right. She'd done wrong. Wanting to save herself from an uncomfortable situation on the farm, she'd sheltered under David's wing. And that had been unfair to David too.

She wiped her eyes and sat down to write to Nyezhiner. She wanted to calm him, to explain that she deeply regretted the whole thing. Her problem was that she wasn't brave enough. Going constantly against the current made her so tired she often just wanted to choose the easiest way. She wanted to hide from hard truths. Even now she knew she should leave the hotel this minute and stop playing the role of David's wife in front of others. But how could she? She couldn't leave Dinaleh here, and she couldn't take her away by force without being an Übermensch or a total egoist, and she was neither. The simplest thing for her would be—to die. He mustn't think things were good for her here. They were very bad. She had thought she was choosing what was easiest for her, but she had actually chosen the hardest way, because now she felt guilty both toward him and toward David. She was counting the days and praying for the week to pass more quickly. She'd had a strange dream last night. She dreamt she had become a widow, but she didn't know whose.

She wrote the letter quickly, a tear smearing the lines, then went to the mailbox. She took a path that would allow her to avoid David and Dinaleh. On the way back, she found herself at the edge of the woods surrounding the lake. The dark shadows of the woods drew her, and she left the well-worn path. She followed the chirping of a bird. The profound darkness of the woods both drew her on and frightened her. But she kept going. What was she looking for? To quiet herself in the blessed calm of the silent trees? To find an answer to the riddles that surrounded her? Or maybe just to escape? She stopped abruptly. She heard a whisper. Her eyes alit on a tree. In the tall grass under the tree a couple lay entwined, engrossed in a struggle as if they either wanted to destroy each other or merge and become one. Two heads, four feet, the naked loins of the woman and the man—they didn't know that Miriam was standing with her hand over her mouth so as not to cry out in fear. What was she afraid of? She knew it was a couple from the hotel. Why was she overwhelmed with a fear of death, violence, creation? An incomprehensible feeling overcame her, and she took off at full speed. She ran to the lake and stood on a rock that hung over the water, staring at her reflection down below. She stood there with her face aflame, her heart pounding. How tangled, how dreadful, were life's secrets. She wanted to cry.

The lake was deep, serene. The sun was high in the sky, mirrored in the satiny surface of the water, but the water's depths remained dark and full of secrets.

Off in the distance, she could see rowboats gliding over the water. A man plied the oars while a woman trailed her hand in the water. Yesterday she too had sat in a rowboat after Dinaleh had insisted she come along. David had rowed and she had trailed her hand in the water just like that woman. She had felt nothing, neither joy nor sadness.

She looked away from the rowboat and again at her reflection in the deep waters full of secrets, strange and frightening. She felt something pulling her to the bottom of the lake. She could slip into the water quietly, without a sound, and . . . she would be done . . . calm, eternal calm.

She shuddered and, frightened, regained her composure and shook off her dark thoughts. She saw that she was here, on the rock, and not there, underneath. She embraced the joy felt by those who have looked death in the eye and managed to escape it. Some part of her had gone down to the bottom of the lake. Now her mood was lighter, as were her steps. She went back to the hotel on the well-trodden path, and something within her sang. (Her changing moods were not new to her. Nyezhiner had more than once been surprised by her leap from depression to joy. He would smile, but he actually liked that quality in her.) As she sang, her voice caressed her, forgiving her for her foolishness more fully than anyone else would have. Now she felt she could dance her way past all her worries. There was no reason to be so downhearted. The sun was shining, and there was not a cloud in the sky.

That same day Miriam wrote another letter to Nyezhiner. She wrote on a sheet of paper bearing the name of the hotel and the lake. The name Nyezhiner hated so much. This letter had a lighthearted tone, almost playful. She told him about her walk in the woods, about how she had stood bending over the lake. He knew she couldn't swim . . . but he shouldn't worry. She was suddenly glad to be here and not there, at the bottom of the lake. Anyway, in three days, she'd be back on the farm. Next time she'd have to consider poison . . . What did he think about poison? Was that a nice death? It was lovely to die young . . .

Playfully, but with a hidden sadness, she sent off this last letter to Nyezhiner from the hotel. The thought that her week in the hotel was almost over, that according to David he wouldn't be coming to see Dinaleh again this summer, contributed to her cheerful mood.

For the past few days, David had held himself aloof from her. During the first few days, when the two of them spent time with Dinaleh, he imagined they could come together again, but now he felt embarrassed by the thought. Nyezhiner's letters had driven the idea from his mind. The letters surrounded Miriam like a fortress. But this no longer bothered him. Nor did it bother him that Miriam had stopped coming along when he spent time with Dinaleh. He took Dinaleh to a farm for riding lessons. She liked to sit on a pony and felt not an ounce of fear.

Back at the hotel, Miriam sat waiting for the moment the mail would arrive. She now got letters regularly, every day. Like a bird with a crumb in its beak, she would fly with the letter to her room and read.

"So, my girl, are you suffering there? A little suffering won't hurt. It will make you feel me near you. Oh, I'm so uneasy about you in every way. Uneasy because of the angry letters I send you, the ones I pray to God you won't receive. You know me!

"Well, what now? Soon I won't be working. I'll be free from Friday to Monday, and I want very much to visit you on the farm again. Is that possible? Should I? Write immediately.

"Up until last week, I was feeling healthy and calm. Not today. In just a few days I lost everything I had earlier gained both in my ability to be calm and in actual pounds. Don't laugh. I'd gotten fat. Now—oh, my little widow! We must have sympathy for each other because we've both been damaged by our hard lives. Do you have sympathy for me? I do for you. And it feels lovely.

"A kiss on your nose, on your little white finger. On the tip of your shoe. You won't allow it? Do!

"Write longer letters. *Prashu.* Please. *Pleez!*"

4. On her last day in the hotel, Miriam woke up early. Her suitcase was already packed, but she still had to pack Dinaleh's. She had brought little with her, but she was going back with a lot of toys and other things David had bought for their daughter. Yesterday Dinaleh had done something silly: she had let one of her shoes go swimming in the lake. The shoe didn't come back. Miriam wasn't there, and the shoe was lost. Dinaleh had probably learned a lesson. But right after breakfast they had to go to town and buy her a new pair of shoes. Miriam would have to go with them because she had to make sure the size and style of shoe were appropriate. David had never concerned himself with such things.

In the small-town general store, which sold everything from tar to dolls to wagon wheels, Dinaleh ran around pointing at everything. Another doll, another toy. David gave in to everything. Miriam didn't want to interfere. Dinaleh instinctively felt she could do anything she wanted, and she seized the moment. During the week she had become pampered, even spoiled.

On the way back to the hotel, Dinaleh remembered that her

Papa had promised to show her the highest mountain and had not kept his promise.

David looked at his watch. "There's still time."

Miriam said nothing. She didn't want to say no again when David said yes.

David turned the car around, saying the detour would add only a few miles to the trip. The car climbed and a panorama appeared of all of Sullivan and Ulster counties, their hills and valleys wreathed in floating white clouds. The car climbed even higher. Dinaleh was happy. All three were quiet. How good it was that this was the last day, Miriam thought. Perhaps David was thinking the same thing. He was driving at 60 or 70 miles an hour. It was a narrow road, cut into the side of a high mountain. The car could have slid down at any moment, could have rolled off the slope into a deep chasm. But none of them thought of that. They were all strangely calm. Whenever David turned the wheel sharply at a bend in the road, Dinaleh squealed happily.

They got back to the hotel in one piece. David carried up the things Dinaleh had bought, and Miriam went to ask about the mail. The hotel manager brought out several letters. Only one of them was for her, the others for David. Among them Miriam noticed an unfamiliar woman's name and return address. She caught herself looking curiously at the name, glad David wasn't there to see her.

The lunch bell rang, and Miriam went to the dining room to wait for David and Dinaleh. She gave him the letters and saw him separate that one from the others. He put it into his vest pocket without opening it, no doubt to read it later. He opened and read the other letters right away. Now they were equal, Miriam thought, and something felt strange between them. "Dinaleh's face has both our smiles," Miriam said to herself. "And years from now, our grandchild will also have both our smiles. Strange . . ."

David pushed in Miriam's chair as she sat down lost in thought, paying no attention to where she was.

Their last meal in the hotel passed quite happily. The plates, forks, spoons clattered. David wiped his mouth with a napkin and said:

"Well, time to pack up."

››››‹‹‹‹

For a moment, Miriam sat looking at nothing. Less than a year had passed, but she asked herself if she hadn't grown much older during the time she and Nyezhiner had been together. Hadn't he turned her fate around, pointed her thoughts in a new direction? Without him, what would she be feeling or thinking now? What would she have to live for?

In the next moment her gaze returned to the line in the letter before her. No, she had to go back to the very beginning. She smiled at his first line. It was a response to her half joking, half sad letter. (Here at the hotel, the mail came much more quickly than on the farm.)

"Beetle! So you think it might be a good idea to poison yourself? I'll write a requiem in your honor, a poem in celebration of your lovely young death. I won't mention the poison. Feh. Poison is not a lovely death. My girl, do you really want to die? You must be lying. Go ahead and laugh. I'm laughing too.

"Listen, I think I'll be off work from Friday to Monday. Should I come? Oh! Tell me how much money I'll need. Beetle, tell me the truth, do you like me? Do you love me? Do you love me so much that you can't spend a day in those damn mountains without longing for me, that you see me in the highest mountain and in the smallest hill on which you stand with clasped hands? Oh my! You see me—forgive me—wherever you set your little foot. (And what size shoe do you wear? Should I send you some shoes?) Stand on the hill, but don't put your foot on me, on my poor neck where you like to put your sweet little hand under my collar. My girl. Kiss me here, where your hand likes to wander. Beetle, poison yourself, and now I really am in tears—over nothing. I'm crying as if . . . but for no reason.

"I want to write a poem about a white bird that comes to me at night to tell me something intimate and lies down at my side to die. If I can pull it off, it will be a good poem. For now, a kiss here and here and . . .

"Be well."

It was after sundown when Miriam and Dinaleh arrived back at the farm in David's car. When he took the suitcases and the bags of toys out of the car, his first impulse was to carry them upstairs to their room. But he stopped himself. For a moment, a shadow passed over his face and then suddenly he said: "Well, it's getting late."

When Dinaleh jumped into his arms, he felt somewhat embarrassed to show his love for his child. He got quickly into the car. Miriam stood open-mouthed, unable to find the right words. The car turned around and left the yard, and only then did she find the words she could have said.

« CHAPTER 14 »

1. IT WAS GOOD to lie in the hammock under the branches of the old tree. To lie and listen to how the quiet dripped like water over the surrounding valleys and mountains, washing away all the refuse of her disturbed yesterdays and leaving her cleansed and rested. In the monotonous quiet that enveloped the farm, Miriam now found the calm that had eluded her before. The letters from Nyezhiner had also grown calm, quiet, as if the quiet and calm of this place had reached him in New York. He had apparently forgotten the previous week when she had been with David in the hotel. In his short letter, he wrote:

"It's hot here in the city. Very hot. I am counting the days until I come to you. But listen, my Soreleh has been ill. She had an ear infection. The doctor opened the abscess and it's getting better. She's already playing outside. But it has made my heart heavy. I want to come to you, to spend a sweet time together. You understand the situation. But I'm planning to come this weekend anyway because I very much want to be with you."

Miriam answered that same day.

"Come, and be sure to bring Soreleh with you. Have you forgotten our conversation? Dinaleh and I haven't forgotten. We talk about it every day. Bring her here. Dinaleh is eager to see her. After her week at the big hotel, she's lonely on the farm and doesn't know what to do with herself. She doesn't want to play with the two little farm girls anymore. Soreleh will come at just the right time. It will be good for both of them. And it will be good for me to take care of another child. I'll be busier and not so sad. I'll be good to Soreleh. You can be sure of it, even though I can't know my feelings in advance. After all, I don't know what feelings you have toward Dinaleh either, but you're always good with her. You always take Dinaleh's side when I get mad at her, and I'll be just like you. Often I think that I'm at least a bit like you but with the kind of likeness when one face is truly nice looking and the other not so much.

"I've gone on too long and I don't know if I've said what I really wanted to say. At another time I would have torn up these words and exchanged them for something more concise and appropriate. Not today. Today I want to talk, even chatter, probably because I haven't spoken to anyone in a long time. Forgive me."

Letters came and went, becoming a little shorter, like the late-summer days. The grass underfoot was more worn now, yellower. The eye could wander far away over the harvested fields. But as Miriam walked through those fields, her eyes were always focused on the letter she had just taken out of the mailbox.

"Thank God for your recent letter. Beetle, do you know you're beautiful? I just realized it now! Don't you believe me? Believe it! You are beautiful, and that's no lie, and I love you and that's no lie either. I'm afraid to tell you too many good things because they'll go to your head.

"I long for you terribly. I was so looking forward to coming to you this weekend! But I can't come. Soreleh needs to see the doctor again this week. I'll come the following weekend and bring her with me. I don't know exactly when. It depends. So don't wait for us at the train station. I'll check in at Sophie's Hotel, leave my bags, and run up to you on the mountain! Oh, in a reckless moment, I bought myself a summer suit. A light-colored one!

But I won't put it on until I come to you. Do you love me? Yes! I am kissing every little finger of yours."

›››‹‹‹‹

In the subway on the way to the main New York train station, Nyezhiner held Soreleh's hand. For Miriam he was wearing his new, light-colored summer suit for the first time. Usually when he put on a new piece of clothing he felt a kind of lyrical excitement. This time, though, he was not concerned with himself but with Soreleh. She sat quietly at his side, a bit frightened to be traveling for the first time somewhere far away with her father. Hershele had gone to see Chana on Nyezhiner's behalf, and he'd had a difficult time of it. Until the very last minute Chana had been reluctant to let Soreleh go to the mountains with her father. Hershele had argued with her for a long time, explaining that Soreleh needed the fresh mountain air. Finally he'd taken her out of the apartment just as she was, in the clothes she was wearing. Nyezhiner had bought her new clothes and a new suitcase.

In the hustle and bustle of the big train station, Soreleh clung to her father. On the train he bought her all sorts of snacks, but she wouldn't touch them. The train began to move and she looked out the window, fascinated by all she could see. Soon the train left the city, and fields and meadows flew by. A bit farther cows were grazing. Real live cows that she was seeing for the very first time. She pressed her face to the window.

Nyezhiner opened a book and became so absorbed in his reading he forgot Soreleh was at his side. After a while he startled guiltily because he had been so lost in himself. He hugged Soreleh and asked her to try the sweets, but she shook her head.

The train ran farther through the fields, past lakes and woods. Other children on the train made themselves at home and played together, but Soreleh sat clinging to her father as if afraid of losing him.

After three hours, they stopped at a station and got into a car, and now Soreleh began to enjoy herself. She felt all grown up, older than her brothers and sisters, and she held her head high, proud to be out in the world with her father.

2. The lobby of Sophie's Hotel was full of suitcases and boxes. Some guests were leaving, new ones arriving. Sophie looked up at Nyezhiner with her pale little eyes. She hadn't known he was bringing a child. "Is the child the gentleman's?" she asked. "Is she staying here overnight?"

"Oh, no, just for lunch, if possible. Soreleh, look at the lady!" He gently lifted her chin. "This is my daughter. She's been invited to stay with friends on a farm not far from here."

Sophie saw to it that a table was prepared for the two guests who had come too late for lunch. She called for a clean tablecloth. When they sat down at the table—the only ones in the large dining hall—Sophie was eager to speak with them. Indeed, she often did go to the tables to chat with her guests. But this time she didn't. Somehow this guest was different. What was different about him? she asked herself. Why didn't she dare approach him?

She didn't go over to him, but she was quite curious to know why he was there alone with the child. Where was the child's mother? Was he a widower? A widower with a child? What a pity. Well, she was divorced without children, so she didn't have it so good herself. Lonely as a stone. Her ruddy-necked wretch of a husband had been unable to give her children. Here was a refined young man with a polite child. The rabbi back in her Galician hometown had also been a refined man with a house full of children. But she had not been lucky enough to attract such an upstanding man. Only oafs and scoundrels had pursued her. Why did she think he was a widower? Because he was here alone with his child? Who was that woman up on the mountain? Why had she reserved a room for him? Something wasn't quite right here. She had to find out. Oil must rise to the top. The truth will come out. Not all who look refined are truly righteous.

The waiter brought a tray full of food: chopped liver, green olives, red tomatoes, slices of challah, roasted sweetbreads. The silver cutlery and the white napkins shone. Soreleh withdrew into herself. Her cheeks grew paler. She had been with her father in the automat and the cafeteria, but she had never seen anything like this. It was like a movie. The large hall, the tables and lamps, the waiter running back and forth—all this both entranced her and made her feel out of place. Her eyes opened wider. Her mouth clenched tighter.

"Eat, Soreleh. You need to eat to make your cheeks red. Come on!"

He felt helpless around her. She was all nerves. She could be as stubborn as he was. He had to tread carefully. "Just eat a little at a time," he coaxed. "Like me. See?"

My God, what would he do if he had to take care of children all the time? It was one thing to tell them a story, hold their attention. Then they were putty in his hands.

"Listen, Soreleh, once upon a time . . ."

Soreleh opened her eyes even wider. Her lips parted.

The waiter ran over with another tray. Chicken, kugel, carrot stew, strudel, compote.

Nyezhiner took Soreleh's spoon and began to feed her. But when she realized what he was doing, she blushed and took the spoon from his hand.

"That's it. Eat a little at a time and listen. This story is very funny."

He murmured into Soreleh's ear. She suddenly began to smile, opening her mouth with its missing tooth. Engrossed in his story, he didn't notice that she had relaxed and was eating with tiny bites.

Later, Sophie stopped them in the corridor.

"Say goodbye, Soreleh," he said, and waited.

"The child takes after the gentleman. Two identical drops of water. How old is she?" Sophie asked, trying to start a conversation.

"She's eight."

"She needs fattening up."

"You're right," Nyezhiner agreed. He bowed and said goodbye. Soreleh copied him, bending her knees.

"A polite child. Just like her father."

Sophie smiled. Through the open door, she saw them cross the bridge and head up the mountain.

3. It would be good to have a swing here for the children, Miriam thought. She vividly remembered the joy of swinging high in the air when she was a child. Even today, she would have liked to swing high with the same enthusiasm and pleasure. Maybe she could ask the farmer to hang a swing on the old tree? No, she was sure he wouldn't do it. The farmers here were suspicious of any form of enjoyment. There were no swings to be seen. The children on the farms rarely had playthings of any kind. But Dinaleh had more than enough toys to share with Soreleh. What kind of child was Soreleh?

"Here they come!" Dinaleh called out.

Nyezhiner and Soreleh came into the yard. He put Soreleh's suitcase down on the grass and wiped the sweat from his brow. He bowed to Miriam, wanting to hug her, to feel her trembling warmth. Instead he took her hands in his. Their eyes caressed, searching. Miriam didn't fail to notice his new suit. He could see it in her smile.

"Do you like it?"

"Very much!"

He did not let go of her hands. He was about to bring them to his lips, but Miriam quietly warned: "The children."

He had forgotten himself. He let go of her hands.

The children looked at each other with great curiosity. They faced off with the watchfulness of two small animals ready to sniff each other or to fight. Nyezhiner put his arms around them both.

"Soreleh, Dinaleh, you've finally met! Look, you're both the same height!"

"Let's measure!" said Dinaleh, standing back to back with Soreleh.

Nyezhiner touched the top of their heads with his hand.

"Exactly the same height!"

He did not point out that Soreleh was almost a year older than Dinaleh. She was as thin as a rail and green as a leaf. He stifled the jealousy that rose in him.

"Why are we standing here?" Miriam said. "Let Soreleh change her clothes, and I'll make us something to eat. Which train did you come on?"

"Don't prepare anything. We came on the three o'clock train, checked in at the hotel, and had a meal fit for a king."

They were standing under the apple tree in the farmyard. Nyezhiner couldn't take his eyes off Miriam.

"You look wonderful, despite all your little problems."

"You mean the problems at the hotel last week? I've already forgotten about them."

A cloud passed over Nyezhiner's face. It was foolish, comical to be jealous of David. And yet . . .

Miriam took his hands and looked into his eyes. He stood before her like a boy, entirely under her sway. Then she felt Soreleh's eyes on her and quickly dropped his hands.

"Dinaleh, take Soreleh up to the room, show her your toys, and let her choose one of your dolls for herself. You remember what we talked about. Soreleh is your guest!"

Soreleh hesitated, not allowing Dinaleh to take her hand. Nyezhiner picked up Soreleh's suitcase and took her up to the room. Miriam went to the kitchen for some food to bring up, but Nyezhiner stopped her.

"Just put the snacks out on the bench. The children are coming down in a minute anyway."

They sat hand in hand on the bench under the apple tree.

"Did you at least miss me? No," he said half in jest, "you're not capable of it."

Miriam smiled. She was pleased by his desire to draw sweet words out of her, words he knew she wouldn't say, words he didn't like to say either. A letter was different.

"Do you need me to say it?" Miriam asked with longing eyes.

"Do you need me to?"

"Yes, I do, very much."

"Beetle!" And he gave her a quick kiss on the lips.

"Here come the children," said Miriam, moving away.

Soreleh was clutching a doll, and Dinaleh was rocking hers in a cradle. Mary and Anne were following them with mouths agape. Miriam saw the farmer's wife open the kitchen curtains and look out.

She turned her attention to the children. With them she knew what to say and what to do. But Nyezhiner remained hanging as if over an abyss.

Dinaleh didn't care about the grownups now. She was deep in the world of make-believe, enchanted by her new friend Soreleh. But Soreleh kept looking at her father, seeing what a child cannot see and knowing what a child cannot know.

4. Tired from her travels and overwhelmed by the fresh mountain air, Soreleh didn't ask for her father before going to sleep. She knew he would be spending the night in the hotel. The hotel in the valley and the farmhouse on the mountain blurred together in her mind, and she asked no questions. She thought she knew everything. Vague ideas about this place and that, this person and that, all glided over her face like filmy shadows until she fell asleep next to Dinaleh in the big wooden bed.

Miriam changed into her nightclothes. She took the pins out of her hair and let it fall over her slender, naked back. She got into bed and stared by the light of the small nightlight at a page in an open book until the house grew silent. All was still. The chirping of a cricket under the floor was a sign that the house had gone to sleep.

She got out of bed and looked out the window. If you look carefully into the night it doesn't seem so dark, especially when the moon, with its round, womanly face, looks curiously down between the trees and turns the grass white.

Miriam crept to the door. She bumped into the vanity table, feeling for the bottle of perfume she had recently bought and then forgotten. She moistened the tips of her fingers with the fragrant liquid, touched her body, and felt impatient to be with him. He was waiting for her under the branches of the tree, from which you could see the dimly lit window of her room. Miriam didn't want to be too far from the children in case they called for her.

Soundlessly, Miriam went downstairs and into the night. The white moonlight followed her, lighting the way. A particular night floated into her memory: she was a little girl, and her mother took her along to the mikveh. There, in the dark water, her mother dunked three times. The candle in the attendant's hand hovered over her. The attendant's pious lips repeated three times, "Kosher, kosher, kosher."

››››‹‹‹‹

In the morning Nyezhiner was late coming up the mountain. Soreleh was already waiting impatiently for him. He smiled guiltily: he'd meant to get up early but hadn't brought an alarm clock and overslept, then came straightaway.

His dark, tanned face looked as if it had been caressed by the night. Miriam, on the other hand, was a bit pale. She hadn't gotten much sleep. The cock had already begun to crow when she slipped back into her room, into her bed. She'd fallen asleep, but soon the sun rose and the children woke up, and she along with them. She'd busied herself with their breakfast, not noticing the time passing. Now here he was, looking a bit lost, as if he didn't belong. They stole a glance, a touch, a smile. The children were always with them. Soreleh snuggled into her father's arms, her eyes always open wide as if she were trying to understand something she both knew and didn't know.

The day began late and ended early for Nyezhiner. He had to go back home that very evening. Tomorrow, at eight in the morning, he had to be at work. It was very important for him to keep his new job, where he'd been for only a few days. He apologized to Miriam, explaining that he wanted to please his boss and that he was working with new energy. He had to keep this job. He had to.

At sundown he got ready to leave. Everyone was quiet and uneasy, and Soreleh suddenly wished she hadn't come and wanted to go home with her father. Nyezhiner pulled her to him, bent down and whispered: "What should I bring when I come back to pick you up? You must want something pretty, so tell me what to bring."

"I want to go home," Soreleh insisted.

He didn't know what to do.

Meanwhile, the farmer's daughters, Mary and Anne, were collecting twigs so their mother could roast corn for dinner. Dinaleh ran to help them. Soreleh looked at what they were doing and the tears trembled in her eyes.

At that moment, Nyezhiner quickly said goodbye and all but ran down the mountain. Miriam waved after him.

5. Soreleh's face grew round as an apple. But her cheeks remained stubbornly pale. Her face still looked green. She liked to play in the shade under a tree, and she convinced Dinaleh to join her there. Dinaleh liked to run through the fields and climb trees. But now she played make-believe with Soreleh. The game was one that Soreleh had not actually invented but adapted from the fairy tales both children knew so well. Soreleh chose the most dramatic roles for herself, leaving the evil villain roles to Dinaleh.

Both children were well-suited to their roles. Dinaleh, the witch of the woods, stood firm when Soreleh cried hoarsely and begged not to be cooked in a pot and eaten. She pretended to bundle Soreleh into a sack and carry her off to the woods.

The children played well together, but once the game was over, Soreleh sometimes withdrew and stopped talking to Dinaleh altogether, locking her lips as if she were angry. Sometimes Soreleh kept silent all the way until bedtime, and the two children would fall asleep back to back.

Miriam knew they would get up in the morning refreshed, having forgotten all about their argument, but the next day the same thing would happen again. Soreleh was thin and temperamental, like her father. Miriam predicted that when Soreleh grew up, a man would fall in love with her exactly because of her capricious temperament. Who knew the secrets of love?

It was good that Miriam was busy with the two children, because that way she didn't have time to think about herself and wonder about Nyezhiner's letters, which must have been delayed. Or . . . ?

A bundle of newspapers and several letters arrived all together. There was a separate letter for Soreleh from her father, written in Yiddish, with short lines and silly rhymes to make Soreleh laugh. But Soreleh couldn't read Yiddish, so Miriam read it for her. There was a rhyme about "a girl so cute / with no front toot'."

For the first time at the farm, Soreleh smiled widely, covering her mouth to hide the gap where the tooth had fallen out. Then she hid the letter away.

The children went to swim in the woods, and Mary and Anne went with them. On the way Miriam read the letter that had been sent first, according to the date on the envelope. It had been en route for three days. (Such things had happened before.)

"Well, I'm back in the city. Today is a strange day for me, very strange. Wherever I go, I feel you with me. I can smell your presence, the aroma of calm, greenery, and a whiff of perfume. Silly one, perfume is for the city, not for you. What do you need it for? Well, ha, ha, Beetle. You're not angry? Good, I'm glad. And thank you for waving so beautifully when I was running down the mountain. I'm not at all worried about Soreleh. All the way home yesterday, and all day today, I could sense many poems inside me. I'm going to write them down now. Be well, Beetle! Don't miss the city until it's time. I love you like a seventeen-year-old boy, and you, my girl, can't stop me. Don't worry about a thing. Did you catch the kiss I threw up the mountain to you?"

Miriam smiled to herself. "Perfume is not for you. What do you need it for?" Yet he had kept the memory of her aroma with him all day, perhaps because of the perfume that he claimed wasn't for her. Did people really understand themselves? Why had she suddenly become sad?

The children were dancing in a circle. Soreleh was directing the game. The soft rays of the afternoon sun stole through the pines and danced playfully with the children.

Miriam stretched out on the mossy bed under a pine tree and read the second letter.

"I went from work to the café. I spoke with a few people. I didn't eat. Now it's ten at night, and I'm very tired. And, listen, it's been three days since I last saw you. It's good I'm so busy at work. I'll have to take care to keep my job. I have to be at work at eight every morning. And meanwhile I worry that a so-and-so like me has to spend my days in this cursed sweatshop. I must control myself every minute so as not to lose the job. Cry? No, no! I've already cried ninety-two times, according to the accounting of my editor, Olgin. And I kiss you, my one and only, here, and here, and here, on your finger, on your . . ."

« CHAPTER 15 »

1. THE LAST APPLES had fallen from the tree and were rotting in the grass. The biting flies were everywhere. The empty corn stalks were drying in the fields, and Miriam thought about how quickly the summer had passed. So quickly! As terribly quickly as Nyezhiner's last visit, when he'd come to take Soreleh home. They hadn't managed to discuss much of anything. Soreleh never left her father's side. Their stolen hour at night under the tree had been silent and constrained. Miriam had been anxious about the children. It seemed to her that Soreleh wasn't asleep. She had just closed her eyes and would open them as soon as Miriam crept out of the room. Then she might wake up Dinaleh, and the farmer and his wife would hear them. It was clear that what they were doing was no longer secret. The farmer's face had grown harder, as if he were saying, "Enough with you city folk. The summer is ending. It's time for you to go."

Everything—hiding from the children and from the farmer and his wife—had made their last visit silent and confusing. On top of that, red-headed Sophie had watched them carefully with her little eyes, which seemed to be saying, "Oil must rise to the top."

When he arrived, Soreleh, Dinaleh, and Miriam were waiting for him at the train station. They saw him come out of the train all dressed up, smiling, his bag under his arm. They all surrounded him. He patted both children on the head, bent down to kiss Soreleh and give her regards from the other children, asked how she was doing, questioned her, said how delighted he was with how she looked, all the while exchanging smiles with Miriam.

Soreleh hardly said a word. She watched her father carefully with wide-open eyes. Nyezhiner sensed her watchfulness. He took her hand and didn't let it go.

Dinaleh pretended not to care. Why should she? She had her own father! If she wanted, he would immediately come with his car. He would drive her around, and she wouldn't take Soreleh along.

The four of them got into Sophie's car. Nyezhiner suggested they eat lunch at the hotel. Miriam hesitated. But she remembered the farmer with his hard, dry face, who could no longer stand these guests, and she gave in.

Red-headed Sophie, with her freckled cleavage showing, smiled at Nyezhiner as if he were an old friend. She stopped Soreleh, stroked her hair, and said to Nyezhiner, "The child looks better, may she be spared the evil eye."

She gave Miriam an unfriendly glance. Miriam was used to such looks from women. Still, for a moment, illogically, vaguely, as impossible as it was—she was jealous of the freckled woman. She was surprised by the feeling, embarrassed by it, wanted to hide it from herself. She comforted herself with the thought that no one could read it on her face and that soon she herself wouldn't remember it.

After lunch, Sophie stood by the wide-open door of the dining hall wearing a fake smile. A man with a sunburned face, a hairy chest, and a toothpick in his mouth stopped in front of her and wanted to chat. But Sophie turned to Soreleh. "I think your name is Soreleh? Yes?"

Soreleh nodded.

"Do you like it on the farm, Soreleh?"

Soreleh was silent.

"Where do you live, Soreleh?"

"In Brooklyn."

"Do you have brothers and sisters?"

"Yes."

"Where are they?"

"At home with Mama."

"Oh?"

Sophie wanted to keep Soreleh a bit longer, but she saw Nyezhiner coming down the stairs after he'd gone up to get his cigarettes.

She let Soreleh go.

Outside, on the way to the farm, Miriam kept her head down, and Nyezhiner sensed something was wrong. "What is it?" he asked.

She answered very quietly. "That Sophie . . . she was questioning Soreleh."

Nyezhiner's eyes became piercing, sharp, his chin stiff and pointed as if he were facing down an enemy. But quickly he broke into a smile.

"So what, you silly thing," he said with a wave of the hand. "That's just how it is. What do you expect? Of course people will talk, question, interrogate. Can't you just laugh it off? Look at me, Beetle!" He lifted her chin, even though Soreleh was watching. "See how I'm smiling? You should be smiling too. It's a beautiful world! Oh, how beautiful!"

"If only I could rise above it all the way you do."

"You have to. It's impossible otherwise. People don't mean anything bad. What do they know about our lives anyway? Nothing. They know nothing. Do you understand?" And he looked into her eyes.

››››‹‹‹‹

That Saturday night was an unusual one for Nyezhiner. Miriam was anxious about everything, including the children. Lying in his arms under the tree she was on edge, listening. Then she got up quickly and left him lying there alone. But her warmth lingered on his jacket, at his side. He'd lie here a while. Just a short while with his eyes closed like this and let the white moon shine down on him through the branches. Then he would steal away like a thief down the narrow path to the hotel. Just one more minute . . .

He awoke when the first rooster crowed. In the east, between the two high mountains, a blazing red dawn appeared. Milky veils of mist were rising from the valley. The grass was wet. He shivered.

He got up tingling with the morning cold and hurried to the hotel before the morning bustle began. The hotel's doors were kept open all night for guests like him who came in late.

In his room he got under the covers without bothering to undress. He was worried about sleeping too long and leaving Soreleh standing by the path waiting for him. He also wanted to spend a bit more time with Miriam and read something to her. Who knew if there would be time when the children were always with them? He and Soreleh were leaving right after lunch.

He began to murmur to himself the poems he wanted to read to Miriam. His murmuring lulled him and, half awake, he had something like a dream. Chana stood near him, small, wan, old before her time. With her full lips, she was wordlessly demanding something of him, arguing, weeping. Then other women surrounded her. They stretched their hands out to him, and they too were asking him for something, demanding . . .

The women encircled him, and his voice resounded over them like the tolling of a massive bell. And the bell rang out lines of poetry in which every one of them was named. And the women bent down and lifted up the lines, the rhymes, the words, as if they were golden coins. The figures of the women melted away and the bell pealed: "Now it is autumn, my autumn, and I have nothing more for any of you."

He tore himself out of the dream and heard an actual bell ringing. It wasn't the thunderous tolling from his dream, just a little bell tinkling on the hotel veranda, waking the guests for breakfast.

He washed, shaved, and changed his clothes, and the dream hung over his eyes like a fog.

He went to the open window and breathed in the crisp mountain air. The mountains rose out of the mist. On their slopes the red rust of autumn was climbing and spreading. The tall oaks with their copper crowns stood stiffly along the dusty path. A few dead leaves had floated down onto the withered grass, and along the fence colorful autumn flowers were just beginning to bloom—a riot of sun-yellow, blood-red, and snow-white blossoms mingling with the fallen yellow leaves.

It was the beginning of Indian summer, he said to himself. He saw it now in all its glory and absorbed it to the last drop.

2. Soreleh waited impatiently for her father. Her suitcase was packed and she was ready to go home. Among her things lay a doll Dinaleh had given her. The suitcase was standing in the yard, and all three of them were waiting for Nyezhiner to arrive. Soreleh ran to hug him when she saw him climbing the hill. Miriam and Dinaleh stood to the side. Miriam noticed how dapper he looked in his traveling clothes. He looked at Miriam over his daughter's head. He wanted to tell her about his odd night, about his dreams, about the poems he had dreamt about. Maybe they'd be able to be alone for a minute, without the children. "Oh, it's so beautiful here today!" he said. "I want to say goodbye to the woods. Miriam, don't do anything in the kitchen. I've ordered lunch at the hotel for all of us."

"For all of us?"

"Don't you want to?"

Miriam didn't answer. She wanted to spend their remaining few hours alone with him, not at Sophie's Hotel. But she wasn't eager to prepare a meal here either, because the farmer was seldom in the fields now. He was always around with his stiff face, and his wife had turned strangely silent. Miriam had tried to win her over with gifts for her daughters, but she could tell the woman wasn't fond of her guests and was waiting for the minute they would leave.

"Silly one, why so sad?" Nyezhiner said as if he were reading her thoughts. "We can't run away from people, we can't hide, and we don't need to. There's no point. Do you understand? Anyway, we're all going from the hotel to the train station. The train leaves at three o'clock and gets to New York at six or seven. I have to bring Soreleh home early, and by the time we get to Brooklyn . . ."

His brow furrowed. In the corner of his eyes, creases suddenly appeared. He looked into the distance, taking his leave of the farm, the tree . . .

3. Strewn around the hammock lay newspapers and magazines that Nyezhiner had left behind. Miriam tried to read them but soon tossed them on the grass. She swayed in the hammock as if to rock herself to sleep, but her thoughts kept her awake: What was he doing now in the city? Was he anxious about her return? Where would she return to? He had suggested that for the time being she take a furnished room, but no, she wouldn't take Dinaleh to a furnished room for even one day. She had to arrange a home for the child right away. But she couldn't rely on him for such things. He was too impractical to find a home for them. Even for himself, he'd just taken the first room that appeared. She would go home sooner than she had planned. Why did it seem to her that as the train was pulling away he'd withdrawn his face from the open window too quickly? As the train picked up speed along the rails stretching into the distance, she stood watching until it disappeared from sight, and everything around her looked lost and empty. Why hadn't he kept his face at the open window longer? Was it because of Soreleh? And why had she stayed here on the farm? So that she could rest a while

before dealing with all the difficulties involved in her return to the city? She was ready to leave. With every fiber of her being she was already back in the city. She had no more patience for lying in the hammock. She'd go see if perhaps there was a letter from him today.

A moving letter had indeed arrived from Nyezhiner. Among other things, he wrote that he was still staying with Hershele. He hadn't gone to the seaside for a few weeks, as he had thought of doing. He'd thought she and Dinaleh might also want to be at the seaside now. But it had suddenly grown cold, and it never stopped raining. So what good was the seaside? Second of all, he'd lost his job. He was running around looking for another. He had to find one immediately. Meanwhile, being without a job, he had written several poems, simple folk ballads he would send to the newspaper to earn some money. Here was one of them:

Play, klezmer, play me a tune,
Play me a cheerful air.
Play, klezmer, play me a tune,
Release me from every care.
But the fiddler fiddles a lonesome tune
A song that cuts like a knife.
I see: though my own days are painful and sad
He too has a difficult life.

"A simple folksong. Worthless. Still, I felt sentimental while I was writing it. I actually cried. But out of that sentimental feeling came a second poem. One that others may think they understand—but in fact you and I are the only ones who can really understand it, because it's about us."

Not out of wicked or sinful desire
Your hands reach across to grasp mine.
Our fingers like serpents so blindly entwine,
Hand in hand, our longings are eased.

Is it just for today or is it for more
That our hands are so tightly entwined?
I smile, for I hope, I believe, I can see—
Hand in hand ever after we'll be.

"Don't you like it? To me it seems very intimate. When we said goodbye, I felt as if I was inhabiting this poem. Beetle! Do you remember that time when I was in the hospital and the nurse had to draw the curtain because our passionate farewell was disturbing the other patient? Now that we're apart I feel lost. Nothing seems real. Beetle, right now I'm sitting in Hershele's apartment and writing this letter to you. I'm very nervous and it's raining hard and I'm lost. Well, I kiss you like this. Look. And I kiss you with my hand like this . . . Be well and write about everything. Will you be able to arrange everything? So many difficulties, aren't there? So *be a man!*"

There was also an exchange of letters between Miriam and David. She wrote that she and Dinaleh were coming back to New York soon and would stay with Moyshe until she found an apartment. It wouldn't take long because there were plenty of empty apartments to be had. She hoped he remembered they'd agreed Dinaleh would live with her. She would let him know when and where he could see Dinaleh as soon as they got to town.

He answered that he hadn't forgotten a thing. He was always true to his word; she could depend on it. He had promised to support their child with everything she needed, and that's what he would do. Dinaleh would lack for nothing. He certainly wouldn't want his child to be without a proper home. He was staying in the apartment until the end of October. But Mrs. Stein was about to go to the hospital for a gallbladder operation. He asked Miriam to call him as soon as she got to town, and he would bring Dinaleh to his home for supper and perhaps have her stay overnight. He wanted to have Dinaleh with him once a week so she wouldn't become estranged from him. Miriam would remember that this was part of their agreement.

A short, nervous letter came from Nyezhiner.

"You write that you're coming to town. And what about me? I don't even know your plans. I'm worried to death. I need a place to live, but I won't worry you about that. I walked around Williamsburg looking at to-let signs for empty apartments. Just come, and all will be well and I'll follow you and your plans. Are you even thinking about me? If not, things are bad. Write exactly when you're coming and what train you're on and I'll be waiting for you at the train station. And, Beetle, before you start out, don't forget our woods.

"So, be well. My last foolish kiss is on this paper. Write to me this very minute. I'm so worried!"

« CHAPTER 16 »

1. SUDDENLY THE weather changed. Clouds scudded across the sky. Gusts of wind bowed the trees to the ground, and empty birds' nests lay in the grass. Dry leaves swirled in the air. Everything seemed to be saying farewell to the summer. So was Miriam. She and Dinaleh were standing in the yard with their suitcases, waiting for the farmer to take them to the train. He was in a hurry. He'd interrupted his work in the fields, and he had to get the last of the harvest into the barn today, before the heavy rains fell and ruined it. Neighboring farmers hired people to help them in the fields, but he worked alone. His farm wasn't yet paid for, and every penny mattered. During the summer his face had grown even drier and harder. He flicked the whip when Miriam and Dinaleh got onto the cart. His wife and the children, Mary and Anne, stood by watching quietly as Miriam and Dinaleh departed. Dinaleh waved to them. Miriam cast a look at the woods that were visible through the leafless branches of the tree. In her thoughts she said goodbye to the summer days. And the nights.

The horse and cart emerged onto the wide-open road. The surrounding farmhouses, bare of summer greenery, now looked poor and naked. Gray and white houses, red barns flew by. The distant misty mountains seemed stooped under the approaching loneliness of winter.

Miriam was glad to be returning to the city. She remembered a summer, not long ago, when she'd stayed in the mountains with Dinaleh until late autumn because of the polio epidemic in the city. There were no other guests in the hotel, just her and Dinaleh. The tops of the tall trees blazed red, and then the ground was littered with dead leaves. She walked in the dry leaves up to her knees and saw how the wind forced the naked trees to the ground. Her heart was full of fear and sadness. How brutal nature is in autumn.

She never wanted to see such a sight ever again.

Dinaleh's eyes were strangely dark, and she held her doll pressed tightly to her.

As they passed Sophie's Hotel Miriam turned her face away. She still had an unpleasant feeling about Sophie and her hotel. It was strange how fate had brought her there. She imagined that Sophie and all the guests in her hotel were the same as her backward relatives with whom she could no longer speak.

The horse and cart clattered over the wooden bridge. Nearby the ground had been broken, and the cornerstones of a new hotel had been laid. The farmer muttered to himself: "These damned hotels are sprouting up overnight like mushrooms." He tugged on the reins, and the horse galloped over the empty path.

The train was packed with women and children going home from their summer vacations, their bodies plumper, their tanned skin sprinkled with freckles. The women opened bags, ate, and fed their children. The children ran through the train making a racket, with Dinaleh in their midst.

Miriam looked out the window. The landscape flew backward, and so did her scattered thoughts. She opened a book without expecting to read. She didn't turn a single page, but the hours, like pages in a book, turned and turned, and then the train entered the underground tunnel of New York's main station, screeched to a halt, and stood still.

›››‹‹‹‹

As always when she came back to town at the end of summer she found the crowds invigorating. Groups of people and solitary travelers alike flew by as if they were ice skating. Some were greeting one another, others saying goodbye. Crowds surged forward as announcers called out the names of far-off towns. Miriam scanned the dizzying scene but didn't see Nyezhiner. For a moment her heart sank. Maybe he hadn't gotten her last letter? Maybe something had happened and he couldn't come to meet her? She'd go into the waiting room. People always seemed to be sitting there waiting for someone who would not come. All of a sudden he was by her side.

"Miriam! I didn't recognize you. Your face is darker, fuller. A mulatto."

His face broke into a smile. His hat was askew on his forehead, and he looked as if he'd been blown there by the wind.

They looked at each other with a kind of bewilderment. Dinaleh was standing between them, so they didn't kiss. Meeting at the big station was strange for both of them. They hadn't seen each other for four weeks, and in this unfamiliar place in the light of day they looked different. He seemed a bit older. He had a new wrinkle on his forehead. And she had darker skin and a new, round face. Only with the press of his lips on her fingers did they feel each other's presence, recognize each other, and smile—yes, here they were. The same two.

They stood in the middle of the stream of people on 42nd Street.

"Miriam, where are we going? I feel awkward. Here you are. I should have at least arranged for a room."

"It's better like this. Dinaleh will feel at home with her grandmother and her Aunt Freydl. And I can leave her there and go wherever I need to without worrying."

"Are you sure they want you there?"

"I wrote them that I was coming with Dinaleh for a few days. I'm sure they won't throw me out. It's strange, but because my mother is there I feel as if I can go there any time."

Nyezhiner now saw Miriam and Dinaleh as two children, one a little older than the other.

"Don't think I haven't done anything about an apartment. I've asked around and I have an address." He tapped one pocket, then another. "Ah, I left it in the other suit."

Miriam smiled at his absent-mindedness.

"I forgot to tell you," he went on, "I'm working in a new shop. I never work on Saturday afternoons, but I did work today. You know, it's a new place . . . I just came from there now."

Miriam saw he was still covered with dust from the shop. She didn't know whether to be happy that he was working. She knew he was none too happy about it.

"So we'll go to Moyshe's," he said a bit sadly.

They took the First Avenue El and then a trolley from Delancey Street to Brooklyn. After three months away from New York, Miriam liked the noise and hubbub of all the people in the streets. It was good to come back to the big city, but she needed to get used to the grayness of the buildings and the tumult once again.

"Ma," said Dinaleh, "when I grow up, I'm going to be a farmer."

"Very nice. Very nice," Miriam answered as they got off the trolley.

Nyezhiner carried both suitcases. They came to the tall building on the corner where, one night many months ago, he'd stood stubbornly by the wall and a policeman had grabbed him by the shoulder in the dark corridor. He said, with barely a smile on his lips, "I have no luck with that building. It won't let me inside."

Miriam gave him a look he couldn't read. Although they didn't speak of it, he knew her family still didn't want to get to know him.

He carried the suitcases to the fourth floor. She didn't ask him in, but they arranged to meet later.

2. Freydl was the first to hug Dinaleh. The child was dear to her heart. She had coddled her since she was just a tiny thing. If God willed that she should get pregnant and give birth—she had miscarried twice—she would want a girl first. She would talk to her as thoughtfully and calmly as Miriam spoke to Dinaleh and would teach her to play the piano.

"She looks wonderful!" she told Miriam. "And you too. You both look good as gold!"

"Tfu, tfu, tfu!" the old woman muttered as she accepted their kisses. "May you be spared the evil eye!"

The old woman with her wrinkled face studied Miriam. She seemed happier.

"You look pale, Mama," Miriam said. "What's wrong?"

"Nothing, God forbid, nothing. May it continue."

"Don't you ever go out for some fresh air?"

"Of course I do. Sometimes I sit on the stoop for a bit. But I don't have the patience to sit too long. It makes me dizzy, no evil eye. So many people."

"And yet we can never convince you to leave the city and spend a few weeks in the country. You have no idea how good the fresh mountain air would be for you. You could have come to me for a while."

"The countryside is not for me, my child. I've lived all these years in America without it. May the future be no worse. Dinaleh, come here. Let me get a good look at you."

Moyshe came in and greeted Miriam with the kindly smile of an older brother. He was pleased that his younger sister had come back to him. It was a sign that he knew how to deal with her without alienating her. Sooner or later everything might work out for the best with David. Maybe it would happen here, in his home.

When Freydl went down to buy something at the grocery store, Miriam quietly asked her to phone David for her and tell him she had arrived with Dinaleh. She was supposed to call him from the station, but . . .

"I'm going down anyway. It's not a big deal."

"I wouldn't ask anyone else."

"Silly thing, why do you need to explain yourself?"

When Freydl came back, she said loudly, "David will be here at six o'clock. I just spoke to him on the phone." She wanted to let everyone know without Miriam having to say it.

Miriam hugged her with her eyes.

Moyshe was twirling his mustache. He kept his counsel. "Hmm," he thought, "maybe the little one has changed her mind after all." By "the little one" he meant Miriam. Things must be going well if David was coming over.

The old woman's wrinkled face lit up, then darkened again. She muttered to herself. What did a sinful person know? Everything was in God's hands. As Miriam's fate dictated, so it would be. Who was she to argue with God?

But later, at six o'clock, when David—who was always punctual—came into the apartment as if he were a member of the family, hiding his estrangement behind a forced smile, the old woman's heart was torn. A pity. What had he done to deserve this? How had he sinned? He had been home night and day. Become a mensch before her very eyes. What a blessing! But with both her eyes and her heart she could tell Miriam wasn't pleased to see him. Even as a girl she used to grow downhearted when he came to visit, as if he were blocking the door to the rest of the world and preventing her from meeting her true partner. Why had the Almighty made it so? God himself probably knew why. But she didn't, and she couldn't bear to see the sorrow that had resulted from the match.

Freydl began setting the table. "You'll eat with us, David," she said, just as she used to do in the good old days.

David was holding Dinaleh's hand, ready to leave.

"Don't run off," Moyshe insisted. "Stay for dinner."

David excused himself. He'd have liked to . . . but he hadn't planned on it. Mrs. Stein had made a special meal for Dinaleh, and she was waiting for them. He had to leave. He couldn't tell Moyshe that even if Mrs. Stein weren't waiting for them it was painful to stay here, because everything was over between him and Miriam once and for all. He knew it.

Dinaleh clung to her father. Miriam could see that since their separation, Dinaleh had become closer to him. She was suddenly jealous. Dinaleh was on his side . . .

David said goodbye quickly, still holding Dinaleh's hand. Miriam took a light jacket and left the apartment with them.

Those left behind in the house were silent. It looked as if, perhaps . . . perhaps the pair wanted to be alone, to talk things over between themselves?

Moyshe suddenly said, "Who can figure them out?"

For a while they walked down a long block without speaking. David held himself stiffly. Dinaleh stroked his hand, and Miriam saw it, but without feeling the sharp pangs of jealousy from before. After all, she reflected, the child believed he had been wronged.

Miriam broke the silence by asking about Mrs. Stein. Was she really going in for a gallbladder operation? Once again, she assured him that within a few days she would have found a comfortable home for Dinaleh.

David didn't for a minute doubt Miriam's ability to make a home for their child and herself, even under these conditions. It was true that by supporting Dinaleh he was helping to provide for Miriam, too, giving her a secure foundation for her new life. A year ago he would have begrudged her that. But now it didn't bother him. He knew that Nyezhiner would be there with the two of them, and he was prepared for that. Why should he fool himself? He wanted to rebuild his own life too. Once the divorce was settled, he'd remarry, and then maybe Dinaleh would even want to live with him. Time would tell.

Dinaleh would be sleeping at his house tonight, he said without looking at Miriam's tanned face. He would bring her back early tomorrow because Mrs. Stein had a doctor's appointment. She had let him know she would stop working for him at the end of the week. But he wanted Dinaleh to spend one day a week with him. He had a right to that, didn't he?

"Of course!"

Miriam kissed Dinaleh. "Papa will put you to bed tonight," she said. "Tomorrow, if it's a nice day, I'll take you to Coney Island. Good?"

Dinaleh was unusually silent.

"She's tired from the journey," Miriam said. "Put her to bed early." And she went quickly in the opposite direction.

A strange sense of freedom overtook her, a freedom she had been longing for. She felt a happiness tinged with sadness as she went forth into the wide world. A light breeze stroked her face. A pure joy called to her from afar, luring her onward. On the streets and across the bridge, lamps were being lit by an unseen hand. Trolley cars criss-crossed the plaza, their wires sparking. Couples strolled on the streets, and she felt herself a part of the rhythmic thrum of this fantastic city.

She had agreed to meet Nyezhiner in the restaurant where they used to eat, and she found him waiting for her by the entrance.

"Well, how did it go? I mean, all in all?"

"Much easier than I expected. David came over and took Dinaleh with him for the night. Everything went off without a hitch. Perhaps there's really no drama in life except when we make it ourselves."

"You're so smart."

"Smart like a fool."

"Life would be boring without the foolishness of clever people."

"Maybe . . ."

He reached for her hands. Once again their fingers were entwined across the table, just as they had been the first time they'd been here.

"Do you remember, Mira? It's been almost a year!"

Yes, she remembered. She had been staying at Moyshe's house then just as she was now.

The waiter came and she pulled her hands away.

"I have the address of an apartment here," said Nyezhiner, taking a piece of paper out of his pocket. "Julia gave it to me. She was at Hershele's a few days ago. I don't know why I asked her of all people if she knew of a comfortable apartment. Hershele gave me a look, and I was sorry I'd said the word 'comfortable.'"

Miriam looked down.

"You understand that I'm embarrassed to live 'comfortably.' But I'll have to get used to it. Because of you."

Miriam had a sudden desire to say something that would hurt him, but she controlled herself.

"Beetle, do you understand?"

Miriam lifted her eyes to him. Of course she understood that he was suffering under the weight of the guilt he felt toward Chana and the children. But it was not because of her. She was not to blame. She didn't owe anyone anything. Not David, and not even Dinaleh. She hadn't chosen this hard life for herself. Her path in life had been charted against her will, and she'd had to walk it anyway. Her life with David had ended because it was wrong from the beginning. She was still nearly a child at their wedding. But no one was to blame. It was the same for Nyezhiner. He knew he could never go back to Chana. The chasm between them was too wide. It was over. But still he was ashamed to live happily in a conventional way because of Chana and the children. He wanted to punish himself to assuage his guilt.

It was difficult to talk about these tangled issues. Miriam didn't say anything. But in her bearing she conveyed an absolute certainty that what she was doing was right. She had to do it. It was her fate.

She looked at the address and said, "I know this street. Our old doctor lives there."

Before her eyes appeared the doctor's waiting room, his dark office, the room behind closed doors, the patients—all young women. Every hour another would lie in the room behind the doors, holding in the pain and the shame after her abortion. Every woman there was throwing the dice, risking it all in order not to have another child.

Nyezhiner asked, "Before it gets too late, do you want to go take a look at the apartment?"

"Yes, I'd like to."

"The people there have bought the house only recently. Can you imagine anarchists owning their own home?"

"Do you know them?"

"No, but Julia does. They used to be part of her circle."

"Yes, of course, even anarchists have bourgeois tendencies."

They both smiled.

3. They stood in front of a brownstone with a tall stoop. The house looked like all the other three-story houses lining the street except for the two stone lions guarding the steps and the ivy climbing up to the top floor.

They went up the broad steps and Miriam rang the bell on the massive door. After a moment, a middle-aged man with a goatee opened up. He looked like a cross between a businessman and an artist.

"It's about the apartment," stammered Miriam, suddenly feeling anxious and uncertain.

"Oh, the apartment." Maybe they could come tomorrow? Unfortunately, he couldn't give them any information. His wife took care of all that, and she wasn't home.

"Oh," sighed Miriam. "Couldn't we take a look? Since we're already here?"

The man stroked his beard. He looked them over with a friendly smile. It really was his wife's business. She was the one who took care of it. He didn't mix into such things. Still, he opened the door wider and invited them in.

They followed him up the carpeted stairs to the top floor. He opened a door and turned on the light.

"This is it. The entire floor. Three rooms and a bath." His wife was planning a renovation, but he couldn't say exactly what she had in mind. "Who sent you?"

"An acquaintance. Julia Polonski," said Nyezhiner.

"Oh, yes, yes, Julia! I'm Abram Ginzberg," he said with a bow.

They shook hands and told him their names. Abram Ginzberg now remembered seeing Nyezhiner's name in print, maybe in the anarchist papers he no longer read.

They went back down the carpeted stairs. In the corridor, a little girl of eight or nine appeared, and Ginzberg called out to his daughter.

"*Manitshka, idti spat,*" he said in Russian. "Go to sleep."

››››‹‹‹‹

"I like it a lot," Miriam said when they were back on the street.

"Me too," agreed Nyezhiner after a bit. "But . . . there's something . . . I mean."

"What?"

"It's too pretentious. That man—his beard, speaking Russian to his daughter, the parquet floors, high ceilings, a bath with mirrors! What does all that have to do with me?"

"I like big rooms with high ceilings," Miriam said. "I even like parquet floors. Did you see the windows? They open lengthwise, like in Europe. They look east and west—sunrise, sunset! The front room will be yours. All I need is a bed to sleep in. I don't care if the rooms look empty. I like empty rooms. I like things neat and tidy. And look at the street. It's quiet, peaceful, and not far from the school."

Nyezhiner was silent.

"I know you'd rather live in a basement apartment in a slum," said Miriam, smiling.

"Yes, I would," he said. "How did you know?"

"Remember how you said you were embarrassed to be comfortable? I understand what you mean. And I know that, like everyone else, you do like some comfort, but . . . you deny yourself because . . . but my situation is different. I have Dinaleh to take care of. Here, when I need to go to work, I won't have to worry. There's almost no traffic on the street because it's a dead end. I saw a yard behind the house, and there's a child for Dinaleh to play with. Do you know what that means for me? I wasn't expecting to find all this!"

"Well, you know what's good for you. I'll leave it all up to you. You decide and do what's best for you, and I'll follow you the way a horse follows its oats."

Miriam laughed, and they kissed in the middle of the street.

"Beetle, where should we go now?"

"I don't know. All of a sudden I feel tired. So much in one day! I wish I could just lie down," said Miriam, cuddling up to him.

"Me too. With you. Oh, if only I had my old room!"

"It's a good thing you don't. If you did, I'd go there with you and stay overnight. And Freydl has made up the sofa for me, and my mother will keep the door unlocked all night waiting for me."

"Let's get a room for a few hours in one of those rooming houses."

"I don't know. I'm afraid of those things. Maybe we can go to a movie? It's Saturday and they're open late. I'll snuggle with you and maybe fall asleep on your shoulder, I'm so tired."

He kissed the palm of her hand, took it into his own, and then into his pocket. "I don't deserve all this. You've fallen like a quivering dove into my hand."

"That sounds like a line from a poem."

"Yes, it might become one."

He was suddenly lost in himself as if he had forgotten her. He began to mutter something as though composing a new poem. She held her breath, wanting to disappear, not to disturb him. Just now she had been contrary, rebellious. Now she stepped softly, quietly, as if she wanted to be nothing more than a shadow by his side.

« CHAPTER 17 »

1. Mrs. Ginzberg seemed happy to have rented the apartment through a referral, not just to someone off the street. She wasn't looking for people off the street, nor did she like to chat with the neighbors. Just as her husband had become immersed in his jewelry store these last few years, no longer interested in his former anarchist ideals, so too was she busy with the housework and her only child, Manitshke. Manitshke wanted nothing to do with the children on the block. She had no friends.

"It's lucky that both children are more or less the same age," Mrs. Ginzberg said. Maybe they would become friends.

Mrs. Ginzberg spoke a blend of Yiddish and English, but suddenly she began speaking Russian, trying to determine whether Miriam understood the language. Miriam smiled and answered her in Russian. Mrs. Ginzberg pushed a gray curl off her forehead. The diamond on her finger glittered. Her long platinum earrings dangled like little upside-down sails. Her jewelry made her look elegant, but to Miriam it seemed strange that she was wearing it in the morning. For some reason she suddenly remembered the brooch David had given her when she turned sixteen. She'd never worn it.

Mrs. Ginzberg noticed Miriam looking at her shimmering earrings. “This is my husband’s handiwork,” she said proudly. He was an artist at his trade, she said, and she wore the original designs he made for his business. She put on the jewelry early so he could see it at breakfast, and she’d grown so accustomed to wearing it that she felt naked without it.

The two women smiled, and Mrs. Ginzberg gave Miriam a tour of her own spacious apartment. Across from the old-fashioned kitchen was the dining room. The long table and heavy chairs were very old and handmade, she said. She liked antique furniture. But she was going to modernize the kitchen a bit. The kitchen upstairs, in Miriam’s apartment, would also be renovated, with a new oven and sink. “This is the parlor, perfect for Manitshke’s Royal piano.” And yes, every room had its own fireplace.

Mrs. Ginzberg opened a door and there sat Manitshke reading a big book of fairytales. She gave her mother a brief glance and went on reading. Mrs. Ginzberg spoke to her in Russian and, pouting, she answered in English. Her mother told her a girl her age was moving in upstairs.

Manitshke made no response. She sat sedately, with her hands in her lap, looking older than her by eight or nine years. Manitshke was a bit too plump, Miriam thought, and she was spoiled. But Dinaleh would get along with her. Dinaleh could handle all sorts of situations. It was good that Dinaleh was that way. It didn’t bother her to sleep one night on a cot at Moyshe’s and the next night at her father’s. Still, it would be good to stop dragging the child around, settle down, and provide her with a proper home.

Mrs. Ginzberg showed Miriam out, assuring her the apartment would be ready within a week. Miriam breathed more freely. At last they would have their own place. All in all, the apartment was ideal, even if the owners were a bit stuck up. Miriam had felt close to Mrs. Ginzberg when she saw how helpless she was before her one and only Manitshke. At that moment, she’d seemed genuine, without pretensions.

2. Miriam floated in and out of Moyshe's house like a breeze. A week passed, and Dinaleh started school, but the apartment was still not ready. Miriam ran over every day to find out if she could move in. She was busy buying things for her new household. In the evenings, before Moyshe had time to begin twirling his mustache and make his usual pronouncements, Freydl would throw her a wink and say, "You can go." And she would leave Moyshe standing with his mustache wound around his finger.

In those early autumn evenings, Miriam became a frequent visitor at Hershele's house. Nyezhiner wanted her to become closer to his friends. The group of young writers often met at Hershele's. It was there that Miriam met Itche Lichtenstein for the first time. She had seen him from afar, but now he came up to greet her. Standing before her with his back to his friends, he swept his light-blond hair out of his tired blue eyes and launched right in, as if the two of them had been flirting the day before and now it was time to go at it again. His showy monologue made Miriam smile. She felt he was testing her to see if she could follow the twists and turns of his acrobatic mind. In the midst of it all he turned to say something to his friends, who were sitting at the table arguing, and then turned back to her as if he hadn't said a word to them, all the while knowing full well that they had indeed heard what he said and were thinking it over. Suddenly he began speaking to Miriam in a soft, brotherly whisper, addressing her familiarly.

"Your facial features are irregular, my dear. Your nose is too short and your cheeks too narrow. But I find you very striking. Two things about you just kill me: your smile and your eyes. You're just like Carmen: thin and bony."

Miriam threw back her head and laughed. His bold words confused her, made her smile, and disturbed her. She had to parry his flirtatious tone or she would look foolish. She'd felt the same way when she went ice skating for the first time. She knew she had to get quickly into the rhythm of skating or she would fall. Falling on the slippery ice was just as silly as failing in Itchele's eyes.

Heavyset as he was, with his light-blond hair and clever talk, she liked him. Underneath his sharp words spiced with cynicism, she detected a warmth, the kind that reveals itself through a clown's mask.

Once, at Hershele's, Itchele turned to her suddenly, "You know, Carmen herself was quite provincial."

"You're right," Miriam said. "Not a lady of the world or a courtesan in a grand salon."

Itchele stood before her as if he hadn't heard a word she said. He rumpled his already disheveled hair with a soft white hand and asked, "Could you fall in love with someone like me?"

"No."

"Why not?"

"Because . . ."

Suddenly Nyezhiner appeared with that half smiling, half serious look that Itchele elicited with his sharp, playful words.

"Listen, Itchele. You're always making fun of romantics. You don't like them—they're so naïve, so earnest. But be careful, brother. You're tangling with a romantic who can pull a knife."

Nyezhiner was teasing Itchele. Let Itchele see how naïve and out of step with the times he was.

"What should we do with him?" exclaimed Itchele, holding up his two white, Hasidic hands as if in prayer. "He's a lost soul."

Now Nyezhiner smiled. He often played up his own naïveté in order to do battle against Itchele's wit.

Itchele rolled his eyes. With his childish, puffy lips, he muttered a few lines from an old Yiddish poet he was always making fun of. "On an old, broken fiddle, I have played out my life."

Younger than most of his colleagues, Itchele nonetheless acted like an elder, one who knew everything and was bored because he'd seen and heard it all already. Yes, he knew women were fond of naïveté, and so was poetry itself. But he was not naïve. He was full of wit but felt empty of wisdom. His type was on its way out, and that made him sad. Embarrassed by his sadness, he hid behind a light, playful mask.

Once Miriam had found the right tone to use with Itchele, she took pleasure in the clever wordplay with which she could either hide or reveal herself. Every time she ran into him, he offered a playful warmth that neither Hershele nor Yankev Shor could provide. Perhaps it was because he was not deeply in love with Nyezhiner, and so a woman would not get in the way of their friendship. It often seemed to Miriam that Itchele was in love only with poetry. Everything else was playful flirtation. He flirted with countless female friends who sharpened their sophisticated beaks and matched their wits against his.

Once, walking her home from Hershele's, Nyezhiner, smiling, asked proudly, "He's an interesting guy, that Itchele, don't you think?"

"Yes," Miriam agreed. "But I'm afraid of his clever wordplay. I'm always afraid of losing the game."

« CHAPTER 18 »

1. IN THE NOISY shop, stitching a shoe at the clattering machine, Nyezhiner was beset by burning questions: What was he doing here? What did he have to do with the woman's shoe in his hand? Why were his long, thin fingers forever chasing after the shiny needle? Ouch! He mustn't lose himself in thought. The needle had just stuck him in the very fingers that were longing for poetry.

He was forever jealous of his friends who weren't chained to a machine in a shop and didn't care how they eked out a living so long as they were free. He would never be able to do that. He was too proud to beg for money, and poems couldn't provide bread for his children.

Yankev Shor had once told him with a sad smile that it was precisely because Nyezhiner had been chained to the workbench within the gray walls of the factory since childhood that his talent had had to weave its own beautiful new world. Because of this he had become the seeker and the singer of beauty and newness, while his talented colleague was free to spend long hours in the café. That poet saw the world in all its ugliness and falseness and became the cynic who cursed the world and rebelled against it.

"Well," Nyezhiner had answered, "we can entertain such an idea if we wish. But there are certainly deeper reasons why one person's talent develops one way and another's differently." In truth, he often thought with disdain about that colleague with his white, uncalloused hands who played the role of the poet at the café tables. Still, he was jealous of him, and more than once he was drawn to that very table in the café. And sometimes he quit work after half a day and showed up at the café with a smile that hid the urgency with which he had come.

Today was one of those days for Nyezhiner. He was planning to stop work early, and he and Miriam had arranged to meet at the café in the evening. Now his anxious fingers ran faster and faster. The needle flashed without stopping; he stitched one boot after another, and soon he'd be done with his pile of work, while the other workers wouldn't finish theirs until six or seven o'clock. Every day at this hour, when his pile was finished, instead of picking up a new bundle he would want to get his jacket and leave. But he didn't always give in to this desire, because he knew no shop would put up with a worker who shut down his machine and left whenever he felt like it. Yes, it was piecework, and it was up to him to decide when to leave. But the shop had a certain discipline. The machines were all supposed to hum and to stop humming as one.

Nonetheless, he—only he—turned off his machine, and it went quiet. The other workers glanced up furtively, barely raising their eyes from the machines. Their faces were full of mockery, disdain, and indignation. He had the audacity to do what they did not.

He took his hat and coat, glaring at the foreman as if daring him to say something. The foreman turned away without looking at him. They said he was a crazy poet . . . and anyway, the height of the season was over and the slack time was starting. He'd be among the first to be let go even though he was a quick, skilled worker.

Nyezhiner waved to the young woman in the office. She smiled. Oh, the eccentric! It wasn't even slack time yet and already he was leaving in the middle of the day.

Outside the sun shone down, paying him no mind. He blinked

happily, straightened his shoulders, took a deep breath, and reveled in the light, the sun, the air, as if he were tasting it all for the first time. He hid inside himself the golden secret of this golden day.

He set off jauntily, and soon his steps joined with the steps of the city, its rhythm, its current. Where was it going?

In the distance, the sun shone on the arc of the Brooklyn Bridge spanning the East River. Farther on skyscrapers rose like gigantic mountains of iron and granite. He was wrapped in the rhythm of the traffic heading for the bridge. Then he crossed over, and his feet carried him to East Broadway.

There he stood for a moment looking down the street. Of all the streets in the city, this old, gray street was his favorite, with its bearded Jews, its weary bustle, all the dreamers and liberators whose steps were etched into the ancient cobblestones. His steps too? And those of his colleagues? Maybe, or maybe not.

He opened the door of the café, and the poet with the great talent, the one whose free days he envied, came toward him with his smartly creased trousers and his childish, watery blue eyes. Smiling at Nyezhiner with a mixture of admiration and disdain, he combed back his silvery hair with plump fingers, left the café, and disappeared down East Broadway.

2. In a corner of the dimly lit café the silhouettes of men playing chess could be seen. Dense clouds of cigar smoke swirled over the pale faces of the others at the tables. They sat as if in a trance, doing nothing. All the same they seemed connected to one another, as if they were engaged in some endeavor, something that no one had asked them to do, perhaps something entirely unnecessary. But . . .

The waiter stood with a white napkin on his arm, waiting for someone to order something. At the cash register sat the owner, a Jew with a pale East Broadway face and a weakness for books and writers. If he'd had to depend on the writers for business, though, he would have long since had to shut down the café. Thank God for the wholesalers from Hester, Broome, and Orchard Streets who came in between twelve and one o'clock, when the aroma of Hungarian goulash and pot roast was strong. These were Jews with healthy appetites—and cash. The café depended on them. The waiter collected tips from their tables. After two o'clock, when the writers arrived, it was slim pickings. Sometimes the editors of the daily newspapers came in with their important colleagues. They usually sat apart, in a corner, as if they wanted nothing to do with the poets. They themselves didn't talk about literature. Sometimes an editor cast an eye toward the poets as if to say, "What are they making such a fuss about, those paupers? Why are they building such castles in the air? Who can understand those decadents? Who needs their poetry?"

Nyezhiner, the greatest "decadent" among the young writers, had begun to publish his poems in the most important daily paper. But he was paid next to nothing and still had to sit at his machine as before.

When Nyezhiner came into the café, Moyshe Shteinman rose out of the smoke and came over with his cane. "Hershele and Shor were here," he stammered. "They just left. They had to go to the printer. If they'd known you were coming by . . . oh . . . Shor wants to publish Ada's poem."

Shteinman rested his hands on his cane and looked curiously into Nyezhiner's face. Nyezhiner changed the subject, and before they had even sat down at a table Shteinman was already murmuring a line from one of his own poems. Shteinman's lines were like the roots of old trees that were intertwined somewhere underground. He wasn't interested in editing them. One had to take his lines as they were, and Nyezhiner and his colleagues took Shteinman himself as he was. They printed his poems in their journals and regarded him as a sort of "primitive," one of a kind.

A young poet who still had his mother's milk on his lips came over to their table. He sat down next to Nyezhiner and blushed. It was clear he wanted to read one of his poems but didn't have the courage to do so.

Nyezhiner said, "Do you want to hear a poem about New York?" And he leaned toward the two of them and began to read quietly and melodiously.

When he had finished reading, the young poet sat very quietly. After a bit, Shteinman seemed to rouse himself from sleep and all but shouted, "Who else among us can write like that?"

The young poet turned pale, his eyes sad. Alas, now he couldn't read his poem.

Nyezhiner frowned when he heard Shteinman yelling. He didn't take his words seriously, even though often he too believed he was better than all the others. Many times, though, he felt lost and full of doubt, and then it was good to have such true believers around him. They saved him from his doubts, from feeling lost.

It was mostly newcomers who gathered around Nyezhiner's table. Minor poets and writers with young, devout faces flocked to him as if they were his Hasidim and he their rebbe. Here Nyezhiner was entirely different from how he was in the shop. All eyes were glued to his face, all ears riveted to his words. Time itself seemed to stand still, listening ardently to the words of the poet. Piety reigned at the rebbe's table.

Now Itchele Lichtenstein appeared at the door. Through the thick smoke, he spotted Nyezhiner's table and furrowed his white brow. He was a "grandson," the last "grandson" of a dynasty of rabbis. He was deeply irritated by freethinkers, and especially by freethinking poets. His thick lips frowned, yet still he made his plodding way over to the table.

Moyshe Shteinman got up from his seat with an expression on his face that suggested he had something very important to say.

"What is it?" asked Itchele. "Which actress let you kiss her hand? What is Toscanini playing, and which writer is divorcing his wife? Tell me quickly because I don't have time . . ."

Shteinman opened his mouth but said nothing.

Itchele turned to Nyezhiner. "Perhaps you know where I can

buy a live hen, one that lays eggs? My wife came back from the country, and the eggs we get here no longer suit her. I'm on the lookout for a live hen."

Thus did Itchele interrupt Nyezhiner's poetic seriousness and the devout attentiveness of the Hasidim at the table.

Nyezhiner lit a cigarette and blew rings of smoke into the air. He knew Itchele's game. Itchele always wanted to bring the conversation down to mundane things. That was his method, his way. Poets musn't wax too poetic. One could talk about mundane things, and a poem could describe the tedium of an average Tuesday. If Itchele wanted to include the tedium of a Tuesday in his poems, that was his business. He, Nyezhiner, would not play along. He would show him that there was not much to say about mundane things.

"You don't need to look far to find a live hen," he said. "Just go to Hester and Rivington Streets. They sell live hens there that lay eggs."

Itchele didn't answer. He made a face as if to say he had already forgotten what he had just asked. He pulled Shteinman aside to a nearby table, called the waiter, and ordered coffee and cake for Shteinman and himself.

Shteinman shook his head. He had already had coffee. He didn't want any more.

Itchele winked at the waiter, who quickly brought coffee and cake for both of them.

Shteinman sat, unusually silent, and Itchele was tormented by regret for the way he had greeted him. Actually, he liked hearing the slanderous gossip that Shteinman served up whenever they met. This was, after all, part of daily, mundane tedium. So why had he tried to humiliate Shteinman? Why was he so full of contradictions? Well, that was just the way he was. People weren't meant to be consistent. Contradictions were what made them lively and interesting.

Itchele looked up. His eyes were now more violet than blue, and with boundless devotion he looked into Shteinman's face. Shteinman obediently picked up his cup of coffee. He had already forgiven Itchele and stopped scowling.

"Shor and Hershele were here earlier," Steinman said. "Shor read Ada's poem."

"I know, I know. He already read it to me. I'm just trying to remember why the poem sounds so familiar to me. As you know, a beginner is a beginner. There's so much that a beginner cannot know. This one knows too much. Shor, that so and so . . . forgive me . . . has forgotten that he is a poet himself. He has become her assistant."

"But Shor is secretly seeing Julia. Because of him, Julia . . ."

"I know. I know everything. It's such a pity. These women will be the death of him."

Itchele nibbled at his cake, licked his lips, wrinkled his nose, furrowed his brow. Suddenly he called over to Nyezhiner: "I just remembered. I know who she's copying. I can prove it."

Of course Nyezhiner knew exactly who he was talking about. Ada would have been more pleasing to Itchele, and to him too, if she'd exhibited less skill, if she knew less about the craft of poetry. But in fact she did know.

Miriam slowly opened the door of the café and took a hesitant step inside. Nyezhiner saw her right away and came over to bring her to his table. Shteinman kissed her hand.

"You're so pale today," he said. "Transparent. As delicate as porcelain."

Miriam thought she was made of much stronger stuff than porcelain. If only he knew how hard she had worked today he wouldn't have said that.

Nyezhiner brought her a chair. Yesterday he had asked her to come to the café at about this time. His heart had told him he would be here to greet her.

"Just for a little while," she said. She had been shopping nearby. She had to go home soon.

"Why are the roses so pale?" declaimed Itchele. "Why do you look so pale, my girl?"

"I washed all the floors in the new apartment today," said Miriam, smiling.

"What did you need to do all that for?" said Itchele, half flirtatiously and half worriedly looking at her and at Nyezhiner.

"We're off," said Nyezhiner, rising from the table along with Miriam.

3. Nyezhiner pressed her arm in his. It felt good to walk this way.

"I could walk across the bridge again," he said, "even though I've already done it once today. But you look pale, tired. Your summer tan is gone."

"Yes, I'm a little tired. I washed all the windows and the floors in the new apartment. I went looking for bargains too. I bought you a desk, a very simple one."

"For me? No!" He stopped in his tracks, then caught himself. "I guess I'm afraid of a desk. Now I'll really have to write. I'll have to write down all the poems I'm carrying around in my head."

He became suddenly joyful. "Maybe the desk will force me to become a real writer! Beetle, do you need money? Tell me the truth! I received a small honorarium for some translations. And don't think I couldn't earn more in the shop if I worked all day every day."

Miriam was silent. She knew he stole half days from the shop in order not to be entirely swallowed up by it. But work he must, because of Chana and the children. Was she an added burden for him? She would strive not to be. She would always have to work. She would not have a child with him. She mustn't dare.

They rode over the bridge and stood in front of the tall building on the corner.

"You're hurrying to get to Dinaleh, so go. I'll be back around nine tonight. Good? I'll wait here, by the stoop."

"We'll go to the apartment together, and I'll show you everything and where your desk will be."

He waved his hand as if throwing a kiss into the air. There was something both joyful and sad in the rhythm of his departing steps.

Miriam climbed the four flights to Moyshe's apartment with two heavy bags in her arms. She had gone to the grocery store so Freydl wouldn't have to run down at the last minute to buy something for supper. As usual when she was carrying packages, she tapped on the door with her foot and waited for Freydl to open it.

Freydl opened the door, but only by a crack, and Miriam could tell she was upset.

"What's wrong? What happened? Where is Dinaleh?" Miriam pushed the door open. Inside was a most unexpected scene.

In the middle of the large eat-in kitchen stood a small, full-bosomed woman, her hair disheveled. She was surrounded by three children clinging to her dress. Dinaleh was looking at them from a corner. Suddenly Miriam realized that one of the children was Soreleh, who was looking at the floor, avoiding her gaze.

Swift as lightning Miriam's mind went to a moment at Sophie's Hotel. Soreleh's head had been bowed . . . Someone from the hotel—maybe Sophie herself—had gotten in touch with Chana, perhaps thinking to help her, and now Chana was standing here with three of her children.

Chana took one look at Miriam's deathly pale face and exclaimed, "Oh, this is her?"

And she went quiet, as if disappointed.

Sitting in her old chair, Miriam's mother, Chaye Soreh, let out a groan. The hand on her knee began to tremble. Freydl, who had earlier been frozen in place, now took both bags from Miriam's arms and whispered, "Go into the other room. We'll manage here without you."

Miriam didn't move. The first shock that had made her deathly pale had passed. Now she looked at Chana without curiosity. She saw that one of Chana's hairpins had come loose from her disheveled head. She saw that Chana was missing a tooth. She saw how the children clung to her dress. What did any of this have to do with her?

"Give me back my husband!" Chana erupted, and her dry, thick lips grimaced.

Miriam didn't move an eyelash. It was impossible, entirely impossible, to connect herself or Nyezhiner with this woman and these children. It was all inconceivable. But then one of the little children raised his eyes, and she could see their father, his exact expression, looking at her.

Miriam's heart tightened. He was theirs. He was with them. He and Chana were both there in each child, in every childish glance. And they were all alien to her. He too. Now, at this moment. What had she taken from them? What could she give them? Oh, God, how she wanted to disappear, to cease being.

"A decent person doesn't take a man away from his wife! A father from his children," Chana wailed.

The old woman's hand trembled more violently on her knee.

"Dear lady, go home. Go in good health," the old woman urged with quivering lips. "Maybe your husband will come back to you. It's not in my child's hands. It pains me to see the mess he's dragged her into. He seemed like such a lovely person. Who can see into another's dark soul? Dear God!"

The door opened and Moyshe came in, home from work at his usual time. Freydl looked quickly at Miriam. She looked terrible. Worse than people who were put into the grave. She pushed Miriam through the door into the front room. Miriam let her. She knew Moyshe would soon send Chana and the children away, and she didn't want to watch. She stood with her back against the closed door, pressed her temples, closed her eyes, and wanted to disappear into nothingness.

"What's going on?" said Moyshe, looking around the room. "Who is this woman and who are these children? Why is Miriam hiding?"

"That whore can't hide from me! Make her give me back my

husband!" Chana looked at Moyshe, her face begging. "Make her go so far away that no one can find her," she urged, her eyes filled with tears.

The old woman moved as if to stand up but then fell back into her chair. Freydl ran over to her.

"Mother-in-law! What's the matter? Moyshe, don't stand there like a block of wood! Send this woman and her children away! Mother-in-law! Miriam!"

Miriam ran into the room when she heard the screams. She grabbed a glass of cold water and splashed it on her mother's face, rubbed her temples, tried to revive her. "Mama! Mama! Freydl, get the doctor!"

Moyshe stood frozen in place. He couldn't move. Only when the old woman began to groan did he stir.

"Goodbye, go, go in good health," he said to Chana as he opened the door.

The children looked around in confusion. At the door, Chana spoke up. "Never mind. She can't hide from me. I'll be waiting for her. Thank God there are good people in this world who will stand up for me."

Watching from her corner, ready to join the fight, Dinaleh wasn't sure whose side to take.

Moyshe closed the door firmly behind the uninvited guests.

A moment later, Freydl came in panting with the elderly doctor after her, his gray beard preceding him. The old woman suddenly opened her eyes, looked around, and moaned, "Children, you didn't need to bother the doctor."

"Ssh, Mama. Be quiet."

The doctor opened his bag and pressed his stethoscope to the old woman's chest for a long time. He checked her pulse. Then he lifted his gentle eyes to those in the room who were waiting with bated breath.

"She'll be fine," he said, giving Moyshe a good-natured thump on the back. "Nothing dangerous. Just an old heart. Let her rest in bed for a few days and she'll be good as new."

"Thank God! Just a scare," muttered Freydl, and she showed the doctor out.

Miriam burst into tears, then quickly dried her eyes. Moyshe looked at her and knew she was crying both with relief over what the doctor had said and also with pain and disgrace over the scene with Chana. As for himself, he felt entirely cheerful. The doctor's thump on his back and his reassurance that there was nothing to worry about, she'd be good as new—all that made everything else seem small and unimportant. He had no desire to scold Miriam. He felt only pity for her now. Maybe it was all for the best.

Later, when the old woman had taken her medicine and fallen asleep, and the familiar sounds of her groaning could be heard through the half-open door, Freydl remembered that Moyshe was probably hungry, and she set the table. As she absent-mindedly put down the spoons and forks, she suddenly exclaimed, "I don't blame him one bit for getting rid of her. I had no idea such women still existed nowadays."

Miriam looked up at Freydl, asking her with her eyes not to talk about it. By coming to the house, she felt, Chana had achieved something. She didn't think she would be able to look Nyezhiner in the face anymore. Along with Chana and their children, he too now felt like an enemy. A wild feeling arose in her against him, and she could no longer make excuses for him as she used to, telling herself that when it came to practical matters he was just a lost child. No, she thought angrily, and once again she couldn't forgive him for Chana and the other women, just as she'd felt at the beginning. She wanted to hurt him. Let him suffer as she was suffering over everything and everyone.

Yet while she was feeling so hostile toward him, she knew he really was lost when it came to practical things and was no doubt pacing in front of the house waiting for her. But she couldn't go down to him, both because of the others in the house and on her own account, because of Chana and the children and what she had seen and heard, which stood between them now and would always stand between them. Why hadn't she understood that before?

Miriam put Dinaleh to bed and lay down on the sofa entirely spent. Behind her closed eyelids, she saw him standing anxiously downstairs, once again unsure about her. Maybe she should go down to him after everyone was asleep. He needed to know what had happened, understand what Chana had done.

In his room Moyshe smoked a last cigarette before going to bed. He sat with one shoe off, forgetting to take off the other. He thought about something, then immediately forgot what. His thoughts blew away with the smoke.

Freydl walked quietly so as not to awaken the patient. A knock at the door startled her, and she opened it a crack. A boy was standing there with a note in his hand for Miriam. He said he'd been told to wait for an answer.

Freydl understood who had sent the note. She looked uncertainly at the half-open door of her mother-in-law's sickroom and heard a quiet, drawn-out moan. Suddenly she was furious. Miriam should be torn limb from limb if she went downstairs to him now. She wouldn't give her the note. She'd send the boy away. Let him go!

But Freydl did the opposite. She went to Miriam, bent over her, touched her shoulder. Miriam jumped up, frightened, thinking Freydl was waking her because of her mother. Freydl put a finger to her lips and gave Miriam the note. Miriam tore through it: "What's happening? It's past ten and I'm waiting. It's all I can do not to come upstairs. My heart tells me something's not right. If you can't come down, tell me why. What is going on? Should I wait? Should I come up? I don't know what to do. I'm anxious and scared."

Miriam took a pen out of her purse and wrote on the other side of his note:

"Chana was here with the children when I got back. We had to call a doctor for my mother. Now she's asleep. I can't come down to you. Don't wait. Everything has turned topsy-turvy for me, and the way I'm feeling now I can't see you at all, and I don't know when I'll feel differently."

Freydl couldn't help following the boy down to the street. Her curiosity propelled her. She had never really seen him, the man who had caused them all such trouble. Once she'd seen him walking with Miriam, but only from a distance.

Now she saw him up close, standing under the streetlamp across from the house. He pushed his hat off his forehead to read the note. Then he stood still, as if struck by a bullet. Suddenly he grabbed the lapels of his jacket, and Freydl was frightened. She thought that any minute now he would tear his lapels right off. She wanted to run back upstairs to the apartment, but she stood glued to the steps and saw him begin to pace back and forth, holding stiffly to his lapels like a drowning man clutching a plank. He was muttering and moaning quietly, and Freydl thought he might well keep on pacing all night long.

She stood for a while longer on the steps like someone who had happened to wander by, and then she went back upstairs.

All night long Freydl saw him in her mind's eye, his hat pushed back, his hand holding stiffly on to his lapels, pacing ceaselessly back and forth.

In the morning Freydl confessed to Miriam, "I went downstairs yesterday and I saw him. I couldn't close my eyes all night. I don't know why my heart was trembling for him. I was afraid something would happen to him."

Miriam looked at Freydl and could tell that her sister-in-law with her trembling heart had forgiven him everything. She knew there was probably no one who wouldn't with a trembling heart forgive him everything. Women in particular—and she herself—would be the first to see that he was a victim, to sense his pain, a pain that was dark and deep but sent forth a light by which one wanted to warm oneself.

4. The old woman got out of bed and barely managed to drag her trembling legs to the old chair, where she sat down, depleted.

"You see, my child, we mustn't give in to the desire to stay in bed or we'll lose our strength. Well, thank God, I'll sit here for a bit, just like this. After all, what is a human being?"

Miriam fluffed the pillows and changed the sheets. Her mother got back into bed and felt the wonderful freshness of the linens and a sweet tiredness in her bones. She looked at Miriam with tenderness and something like pity in her old eyes. It was strange, Miriam thought, that Moyshe and Freydl had looked at her in exactly the same way during these last few days when she had not gone out. Why? Did they pity her because she'd gotten herself into a predicament? Or were they once again hoping that all would be well between her and David?

She stood at the window looking down into the street. In a day or two, she thought, her mother would no longer need her. She and Dinaleh had been unsettled for too long. It was time for them to move to their new apartment. And he? Where was he now? He had not sent her any more notes. Was this the end? Would he avoid her from now on so as not to burden her with his difficult life?

Her fantasies carried her several years into the future. She saw herself walking on a quiet street and him walking toward her smiling and aloof. His eyes were lowered as if to say, "Well, you were too weak—too weak to help me shoulder my burden. It's over. You couldn't do it."

Miriam shook herself. This was all a fantasy. The truth was different. Reality would erase what she'd imagined. No years had yet passed. Just days. And strangely, the poison that Chana released into her heart had nearly evaporated. The shock of seeing Chana and her children—the children whose eyes looked just like their father's—had faded into thin air or perhaps remained within her like a hidden wound. Strange that every new wound he caused her made her feel distant from him only briefly and then bound her to him even more strongly. Or did one love more fiercely the very person who caused great pain? What was he doing now? Maybe he was sick? She knew how he could torture himself. What should she do?

Suddenly David and Dinaleh arrived. David had taken Dinaleh for a ride in his car. He could have just driven her home and let her go upstairs alone, as he often did. But this time he needed to see Miriam, to tell her that in two weeks he would be giving up their apartment. If she wanted to get Dinaleh's things, she had to do so now. He was a man for whom everything had to be done in an orderly fashion, according to a system. When would she be taking Dinaleh's things?

They spoke for a while in the front room with the door closed, and once again David brought up the divorce. All she had to do was not show up in court and the divorce would go through. Yes, he had met a fine young woman and was planning to remarry soon. She need not worry about Dinaleh. He would make sure she had everything she needed. Was there anything else she wanted from him?

Only that he must keep his promise to provide for Dinaleh until she grew up.

"Of course! Are you worried about that?"

"No."

Miriam felt she wasn't talking to the same David. The passage of time had changed him. He had become more serious in his behavior and appearance, more a man of the world.

It was good that he was getting married, Miriam told herself. Once he was married, not just divorced, her story with David would end, and her family would stop hoping. Even now they were still holding out hope, hoping that Malka, Miriam's older sister, might be able to do something. Malka lived in a city out west where her husband owned a chain of grocery stores, and a letter had arrived saying she was coming to New York in a few days. Of course she was coming to deal with her younger sister. Always the family ringleader, Malka didn't know it was too late. If she had known she could have saved herself the trip.

No sooner had David arrived than he was gone. Miriam went out right away and hired someone to move Dinaleh's things to the new apartment. The next day she went through the rooms of the apartment that had once been her home and marked what she wanted the movers to take. Everything was covered with dust, and it all looked as neglected as if long ago a corpse had been removed and its belongings forgotten. Miriam knew Mrs. Stein had undergone a gallbladder operation weeks ago, and now she was in a rehabilitation center. It was no wonder, she thought, that David was rushing to get married. The place felt eerie.

Her little desk was the only piece of furniture she could call her own, because a friend had given it to her as a wedding present. Should she take it? This was the desk she had once planned to give Nyezhiner because he didn't have one in his room. How unknowable the future had seemed to her back then. And now once again the future seemed unknowable. She was afraid of her rootlessness, but she couldn't stop now. This was how it had to be.

She heard a knock at the door. It was the two broad-shouldered movers she had hired. In no time they had carried the things to the truck, leaving the front door wide open. When neighbors in the hall looked in, Miriam ignored them, but then her face turned red. She was embarrassed in front of them, and in front of the moving men, as if they could tell that what she was doing made no sense, that she was adrift like a leaf on the water.

The men drove away with her things. Miriam quickly shut the door, heard the cold, hard click of the lock behind her, and ran down the stairs without looking back.

She was in a hurry. She needed to phone Mrs. Ginzberg and tell her to let the movers in. She wouldn't be able to get there ahead of them. Dinaleh was probably back from school already, and she had to go to her at Moyshe's because Freydl would be busy taking care of her mother.

Despite it all, Miriam strove to display a calm face, as calm as still waters.

5. Miriam told herself she had to get the apartment in order that very evening so Dinaleh could spend the next night in her own bed,

and so when Malka arrived from out west, she and Dinaleh would no longer be in Moyshe's apartment. She imagined Malka holding forth with her hands on her hips, her double chin shaking: "How can this be? How could the family have let Miriam do such a thing?!"

Malka would find out that this time she'd come too late. Her mother would try to avoid talking about it, and Moyshe would stand there twirling his mustache.

Suddenly it occurred to Miriam that perhaps she should bring her mother with her to the new apartment. Since Nyezhiner had disappeared from her life—or so it seemed—her mother would add a bit of warmth to the home, and things would be as they used to be when she was young. Back then, no matter where she'd been, she was always glad to come home to her mother. More than anything, she liked Friday nights, when her mother would usher in the Sabbath. In the immaculate apartment, the Shabbos candles would flicker over the challah covered with a white cloth. The aroma of freshly baked cookies, cinnamon, and special food for Shabbos would fill the room, and they would all be on their best behavior.

Almost immediately Miriam thought better of the idea. She had to laugh at herself and her wild thoughts. Her mother would never live with her, the unkosher daughter, the unclean one. She was as far apart from her mother as if they lived in different centuries. Her mother was wise enough to bear Miriam's transgressions without comment, yet she knew the old woman felt closer to Malka, Moyshe, and Freydl. They lived in her world, behaved more or less the way she did. Her mother was also unwell. The idea was absurd. She was grasping at straws.

Miriam walked along quickly as if driven by her own thoughts. But the closer she came to her destination the more slowly she walked. Here was the wide, quiet street, lit by streetlamps. The two rows of brownstones were shrouded in shadow. The houses with their lowered shades looked mysterious. A man was walking on the other side of the street, his shadow long and bent. Was it him? No, not him. Why had she thought it was?

She stood in front of the house with the two stone lions at the entrance and the ivy climbing up to the roof. Like quiet words, the notes of a piano could be heard spilling from an open window. Were those notes coming from her house?

She lingered by the front door as if waiting for someone. Once again she heard the notes. Yes, someone in the house was playing a Chopin nocturne on the piano. Who was it? Abram Ginzberg? Ida Ginzberg? Or maybe a guest?

For a while she stood on the stoop. The nocturne kept her frozen in place. But then the notes stopped and she turned the key. The door creaked open. There was a new burst of sound as fingers hit the keys once again, and at that moment she realized that he—Nyezhiner—must be here. She had given him a key. He could have let himself in just as she had.

The carpeted stairs absorbed her steps. She couldn't hear her own footsteps; the notes of the piano seemed to carry her to the top floor. She opened the door to her apartment. A white moon hung in the window. She could have turned on the light, but she didn't. Her boxes were piled on the floor. She made her way around them to the front room that was not yet touched by the moonlight. The chandelier did not light up when she pressed the switch; it had no bulbs. But through the tall windows, pale strips of light from the streetlamp entered the room. After a while she began to make out some shapes. There was the desk. His desk. And on the desk, a pack of cigarettes. Her heart began to pound. He was here. How could she have imagined that he had disappeared from her life? Didn't she know that fate had bound them together for all time? It was no use trying to run away or to hide from him. How many times had he told her so?

Miriam stood in the dark room inhaling the smell of tobacco. Her heart beating more quickly, she squinted into every corner of the room—then stopped short. There he was, curled up on the floor, a bundle of skin and bones. A bundle among her bundles.

She spoke quietly, her lips caressing his name. He didn't answer. She knelt down beside him, touched his bony shoulders, his forehead, his cheeks, his trembling mouth. On her fingers she felt something moist and sticky. Blood? Was he sick? Feverish? Was he having another bout of tuberculosis? My God, what would become of him?

Once again she felt his forehead, his cheeks, his lips. Then all at once those lips vibrated like the strings of a violin, and they fell upon each other, mouth to mouth, bone to bone. Hoarse sounds tore out of their throats. Through the rooms of the new apartment could be heard the deep sounds of a man weeping and the thin tones of a woman's sobs. The weepers embraced, kissed, curled into each other's arms. Then it was quiet.

››››‹‹‹‹

Somewhere on quivering white piano keys could be heard the notes of the young tubercular Chopin.

Author And Translator Bios

Rashel Veprinski was born in the town of Ivankov, near Kyiv, Ukraine, in 1895. In 1907, after the death of her father, she and her mother and siblings moved to New York City, where she began working in a sweatshop at the age of 13. She attended night school and read work by Yiddish-American poets. In 1918 she published her first poem in the Yiddish journal *Di naye velt* (*The New World*), and then published poetry, fiction, and articles in numerous Yiddish magazines and journals. Her books include *Ruf fun fligl* (*Call of Wings*; 1926), *Di palitre, lider* (*The Palette, Poems*) and *Lider* (*Poems*) (both in 1964), *Tsum eyntsikn shtern* (*To the Single Star*; 1971), *Dos kreytsn fun di hent* (*Hand in Hand*; 1971), and *Nakhtfayern* (*Night Fires*; 1978). After the death of the poet Mani Leyb—her lover for more than three decades—she compiled his literary oeuvre in *Lider un baladn* (*Poems and Ballads*; 1955) and published a collection of his Yiddish-language letters to her (*Briv, 1918–1953: Mani Leyb tsu Rashel Veprinski*; 1980). She died in New York in 1981.

Ellen Cassedy is a Yiddish translator with a special interest in women writers. Her translations include *On the Landing: Stories by Yenta Mash* (2018) and *Oedipus in Brooklyn and Other Stories by*

Blume Lempel (with co-translator Yermiyahu Ahron Taub, 2016). She is the author of *We Are Here: Memories of the Lithuanian Holocaust* (2012) and *Working 9 to 5: A Women's Movement, a Labor Union, and the Iconic Movie* (2022). Her awards include the Grub Street National Book Prize for Nonfiction and the Leviant Memorial Prize from the Modern Language Association. She lives in New York City and has a website at www.ellencassedy.com.

ANITA NORICH, Tikva Frymer-Kensky Collegiate Professor Emerita of English and Judaic Studies at the University of Michigan, is the translator of *Desires* by Celia Dropkin (2024), *Fear and Other Stories* by Chana Blankshteyn (2022), *A Jewish Refugee in New York* by Kadya Molodovsky (2019), and numerous short stories, among them twenty previously untranslated stories by Israel Joshua Singer (in the three-volume *Collected Works of I. J. Singer*, published by Koren Press). She is the author of *Writing in Tongues: Yiddish Translation in the 20th Century* (2013); *Discovering Exile: Yiddish and Jewish American Literature in America During the Holocaust* (2007); and *The Homeless Imagination in the Fiction of Israel Joshua Singer* (1991).

The translators are grateful to have received a Hadassah-Brandeis Institute Research Award.

The translators would also like to acknowledge the support of Elliot Golden, Rashel Veprinski's grandson, and his family.

The novel in its original Yiddish version, *Dos kreytsn fun di hent,* is available in the Yiddish Book Center's Steven Spielberg Digital Yiddish Library, at yiddishbookcenter.org.

About White Goat Press

White Goat Press, the Yiddish Book Center's imprint, is committed to bringing newly translated work to the widest readership possible in English. We publish work in all genres—novels, short stories, drama, poetry, memoirs, essays, reportage, plays, and popular fiction, including romance and detective stories.

whitegoatpress.org
The Yiddish Book Center's Imprint